MY HEART TO KEEP

A MAXWELL FAMILY SAGA - BOOK FOUR

S.B. ALEXANDER

RAVEN WING PUBLISHING

COPYRIGHT

Chapter 1

Quinn

S ummer was in full swing, and the weather was cooperating. High nineties, humid, and stifling, with no rain in sight. By the time the party of the century kicked off later that night, the weather would be cooler.

I couldn't believe Daddy had agreed to let me throw the biggest bash Ashford had ever seen. *Take that, Tessa Stevens.*

Nevertheless, I was a ball of nerves. I wanted the party to be perfect, and so far, it was stacking up to be. Jack James, a junior at Kensington High, who was one of the best DJs in Ashford, was in charge of the music that night, thanks in part to Emma Maxwell. She and Jack were friends, although I suspected they were more than friends by the way Emma blushed when she talked about him. At the very least, she liked him.

Plus, about forty or so kids were coming that we knew of. Momma wanted to keep the guest list small, but we were teenagers, and I couldn't promise we wouldn't have more than forty, especially when word got out.

Celia skipped alongside me like she was seven again, her breasts bouncing along with her ponytail. "I can't believe your dad is letting you have a party." She skidded to a halt in the dirt outside the barn, sending a cloud of dust billowing around us.

I couldn't believe it either. Daddy hated parties. He felt they brought trouble.

I grabbed a hammer from the toolbox at the base of the ladder. "I promised him nothing would happen."

She snorted. "He bought that?" She knew my dad well.

With the hammer, two nails, and the welcome banner, I climbed the ladder. "You don't think anything will go wrong?" I asked myself more than her. I knew firsthand that fights happened at parties involving high school kids. After all, Tessa Stevens and I had gotten into a fight at her Christmas party a couple of years prior. But Tessa and I weren't enemies anymore, although we weren't best friends either. Still, I didn't have anyone else who hated me, at least not that I knew of.

Celia held the ladder. "Nah. Unless you invited Marcus and Sloane."

I tacked the banner over the barn door. "Of course not." Marcus wasn't a senior, but Sloane was. We were not friends. Rumor was that she was moving, so I didn't have anything to worry about.

"Then you're fine."

I climbed down. "Yeah. The party will be a success." I wanted kids to remember this night, and not for fights, but for the great time they had.

She smiled, her white teeth standing out beneath her tanned skin. "Heck yeah, it will."

We'd been spending time at the Maxwell lake, floating in rafts, swimming, and having a great time since school let out last month. Even my skin was tanned.

I tossed the hammer in the toolbox at the foot of the ladder. "We should set up the tables inside."

The party hall was one of our old barns that we didn't use much except for storage when Daddy had an oversupply of hay or other farm items. As of late, the barn was empty, though. Daddy was about to turn the building into a workshop where he could tinker on cars and farm equipment, something he and my brother Carter loved to do. He'd even promised Carter that he would have it ready for him when my brother graduated college. I believed it was Daddy's way of luring Carter back home. I didn't think Daddy had to do much coaxing. Carter was a homebody, and if anyone loved working on the farm, it was my older brother.

"Wait. I have something to tell you." Celia's light and airy mood had vanished.

"Everything okay?"

"Liam and I broke up."

My jaw came unhinged. "What? When?"

She lifted her small shoulders. "It's no big deal. We called it quits last week."

I angled my head at my BFF. "You sound sad but don't look it."

She sighed, her espresso eyes glinting in the sunlight. "I was afraid to tell you."

"Why?"

"He's your brother. But it was a mutual decision. He's going off to college. I'll be here. We felt it was a good time. And he wants to play the field. I do too." Not an ounce of sadness tinged her voice.

"Do you still love my brother?" Celia had been drooling over Liam since she was a little girl.

"It's not the kind of love you have for Maiken." She grasped my hand. "I don't want you to worry about Liam and me. We're cool. And if, in the future, an opportunity presents itself for us to reunite, then Liam and I will cross that bridge then."

"You sound old. Are you sure you're my best friend?"

She giggled. "I know what I want, Quinn. I don't want to be tied down. I want to date who I want. So does Liam. I also want to explore more of me. I'm excited about filling out college applications. I'm excited about our senior year, making new memories, trying new things for the first time, and I'm excited about being the school's sports reporter. So many possibilities."

I shared her excitement on most of what she'd said, except I wouldn't be breaking up with Maiken. "What new things do you have in mind?"

She tucked her bra strap under the sleeve of her tank top. "I don't know yet. I've never tried liquor. Maybe I'll start there."

I reared back as my mind grappled with her statement. Liquor wasn't the first thing that came to mind when I thought of trying something new for the first time. I was thinking more along the lines of officially becoming a woman. Maiken and I had yet to take that plunge. We'd been dancing around the topic of sex.

"You know how that went down with Marcus at Sloane's party last year?" Marcus had gotten so stinking drunk he'd fallen and busted up his face. That had been the beginning of a tense junior year for Maiken. His brother had ruined Maiken's basketball season because of his drinking and acting out, causing Maiken to get hit by a car driven by Marcus's girlfriend, Sloane.

"I didn't say I would get drunk. I just want to try it. Maybe we should both try one alcoholic beverage tonight. We should experience that together."

I shook my head. "Absolutely not. I have to have my wits about me. You know my parents will be up at the house and no doubt watching from a distance."

Celia rolled her eyes. "Live a little. One drink will loosen you up too. I can see you're already wound tight."

I snorted. "I'll pass." With my luck, one drink would turn into two, and since I'd only tried a sip of beer once in my life, anything harder than that would surely mess me up.

She pouted. "You're a downer. We're seniors. We're young adults. Let's have fun."

I trudged inside and snagged the box of balloons off one of four tables and threw it to my best friend. "I plan to have fun, just not with alcohol."

She began blowing up balloons with Daddy's air pump while I unpackaged the tablecloths. Aside from string lights hanging from the rafters, the decorations weren't that elaborate. In fact, if anyone wanted to sit, they could use the bales of hay scattered along the walls.

Celia flicked through her phone. "We need music." Within a beat, Selena Gomez's voice filled the barn, and Celia sang along to "Lose You to Love Me." She had a pretty voice, and sometimes I wondered why she didn't take up singing.

"Are you sure you want to study communications?" I asked. "With your voice, you could sell records."

"I don't think so. My voice isn't all that great."

"I beg to differ." My phone pinged, and I plucked it out of my short shorts. I beamed from ear to ear as I answered. "Maiken."

"Hey, babe," he drawled in that Southern accent that made the butterflies come alive in my stomach. "You ready for tonight?"

I swallowed. "Why do you sound like you're about to give me bad news?"

Celia stopped singing and gaped.

"Sorry. No bad news. Marcus and I were arguing. That's all."

I bit my tongue. Marcus was the bane of the Maxwell family, the little black sheep in some ways. His rebellious nature was epic, but Marcus wasn't my concern.

"You're coming to my party, right?" I held my breath. I would strangle Marcus if he screwed things up for Maiken.

"I wouldn't miss it," he said. "But..."

Of course there was a but. There was always a but.

Celia pursed her red lips as she prodded me with her eyes.

I shrugged at my BFF.

"Um... Marcus wants to come," Maiken said.

The blood drained to my feet. "Do you think that's wise to let Marcus come to a party? You know how he gets." Maiken had told me Marcus was still drinking.

Maiken let out a huge breath. "He promised he would be on his best behavior. I'll watch him."

Anger seeped into my veins. If Maiken was worried about Marcus, then I would play second fiddle. Plus, the party was mainly for seniors and some juniors, like Emma and Ethan Maxwell, who were my friends. Marcus was far from being my friend. Besides, he was only a sophomore.

Celia shook her head vigorously. Maybe I needed to take Celia up on her offer and have one drink.

"Quinn," Maiken urged. "I promise he won't cause trouble."

If I said no, then Maiken would be mad. The last thing I wanted to do was get into an argument with my boyfriend.

I huffed. "Fine. But if he so much as starts a fight, I'll..." I didn't know what I would do. "And no Sloane." The two together were a hurricane. "Oh, and Carter is home from college. Just so you know." It wasn't a threat. It was just a fact. "I would hate for Carter to butt heads with Marcus." *Or Maiken for that matter.*

I wasn't sure if Carter would be at the party. Knowing my brother, he would be as far away from high schoolers as possible. Still, if he were home, he would be watching with an eagle eye. Not only that, I wouldn't put it past Daddy to have Carter chaperone.

Maiken growled low. "Marcus will be the model partygoer. See you tonight." Then he hung up.

I glanced at the phone as irritation scraped along my sweaty skin. He didn't even say he loved me. We always ended a call with a quick "love you."

I knew Maiken wasn't fond of Carter, and vice versa. The two had butted heads when Maiken first moved into town and took an interest in me.

"Marcus is coming?" Celia asked.

I let out a long, frustrated growl. "I guess so. Maybe I will join you with a drink."

Where Marcus went, trouble followed. I had a feeling I was going to need something strong to take the edge off.

Chapter 2

Maiken

I wasn't sure if I was looking forward to Quinn's party or not. Carter was home for the summer, and I definitely didn't want to see him. Quinn's subtle threat about Carter hadn't gone unnoticed.

Ethan threw the Suburban into park in the lot outside the Thompsons' farm store. Only one spot remained amid the cars packed up and down the country road. Ethan and his twin, Emma, were driving now. It had been a feat for me to get access to the only vehicle our family owned. With Marcus getting ready to drive and our younger brother Jasper not far behind, transportation would be a challenge. Mom couldn't afford to buy me a car, or any of us a car, unless she got the job she'd applied for at a law firm in Ashford. She was returning to work and finally putting her law degree into practice.

Lights twinkled in the barn across the rolling hills. I could hear a faint *thump, thump, thump* of music. I glanced at Quinn's house between the farm store and the barn. I would bet her parents weren't enjoying the loud music, at least not Mr. Thompson. He wasn't exactly stoked about Quinn having a party.

"Seems like the party's in full gear," Ethan said.

Marcus climbed out of the back seat. "I'll meet you down there."

I rushed out. "Wait. Remember what we talked about."

Marcus curled his unkempt brown hair behind his ear, and his tone hardened. "I'm a big boy. You don't have to babysit me."

"Bro, I promised Quinn. And let's not forget her older brother." I'd warned Marcus on the way over about Carter. "He can be a dick even if you're not doing much. So stay away from Carter." Marcus was aggressive by nature. If I threw in Carter, a fight would break out instantly. "And no drinking." Marcus was a second away from being shipped off to military school, or any private school really. Mom had threatened him on more than one occasion. The problem, though, was that Marcus wasn't fazed by her threats or mine. "I'm serious, man. Carter isn't someone to mess with."

Ethan rounded the Suburban and slapped Marcus on the shoulder in a brotherly love kind of way. "Behave."

He rolled his blue eyes. "Fuck off. Both of you." Marcus was nursing a broken heart thanks to Sloane, who had dumped him. "Let me handle my shit the best way I know how."

That was the problem. Booze was his way of dealing with his shit.

"You'll find yourself shipped off to some private or military school in the fall if you're not careful," Ethan said.

Marcus stuck him with the finger. "Like I give a fuck. And not that it's any of your business, but I'm meeting Holly. So later, assholes." Then he swaggered off like a proud brother.

I shook my head.

"Who's Holly?" Ethan asked.

"No clue. Let's just be happy he's not meeting Sloane. Has she moved yet?" *Please say yes.* The best thing for Marcus was for Sloane to leave town.

"Not sure." Ethan pushed his fingers through his cropped hair as we started following Marcus, who was way ahead of us. "But I heard she has a stepbrother who just came into town."

"What does that mean exactly? She's not moving?"

"Let's just drop the subject of Marcus and Sloane, please. We're here to have a good time." Ethan's eyes brightened. "I'm hanging with Jessica Bento tonight. If you know what's good for you with Quinn, you'll ignore Marcus. Let him fall flat on his face. Then Mom will be forced to take action."

My mouth dropped. "How do you really feel? Shit. He's our

brother. We need to make sure he doesn't hurt himself or others. Let's not forget this is my girl's party. Carter is home, and I don't want Marcus and Carter facing off."

I hadn't seen Carter since he left for college, and from what I remembered, the dude was buff, but so was Marcus. He'd been working out in the makeshift gym we'd set up in the barn on our property, and at sixteen, he was all brawn and muscle. Ethan and I worked out too, but Marcus had arms built to lift a house.

A growl rumbled out of Ethan. "Fine. I'll keep an eye on him. I'm just tired, bro. I'm tempted to head off to military school and away from the bullshit. He's driving Mom to a nervous breakdown."

I couldn't argue with him. Mom looked more frazzled than ever. She'd always been a strong woman, but since Dad died, she hadn't been herself. I couldn't fault her for that, though. After all, she'd also buried her sister last year from breast cancer.

"Kade was telling me the other day that Kody, Kelton, and Kross had been shipped off to a private school in the Berkshires their sophomore year for some brawl that had put a guy in a coma," Ethan said. "You know Mom has been reading up on that private school. Who knows? Maybe a school away from home would be good for all of us."

I knitted my brows together. "I'm not leaving. I have basketball." My season had sucked last year because I'd gotten hit by a car. The accident had screwed up my back, and I'd missed several games last year. My goal in the upcoming season was to bring the team to a state championship, to be noticed by scouts from colleges, and to put every ounce of energy I had into playing the very best I could.

No one was getting in my way, and I sure as hell wasn't about to go to a new school and start over again. We'd been doing that most of our lives since Dad had been in the military. Sadly, Dad had been killed in a mission gone wrong.

Regardless, Mom needed my help, and as long as I could help her before I went off to college, I would.

Ethan tucked his hands in his jeans pockets. "Does Quinn know you're going to basketball camp for the rest of the summer, by the way?"

I bit my lip. "Nope. I haven't had a chance to tell her." In all fairness to me, I'd just found out I could go. Mom had needed to look at the budget before she could say yes or no. Apparently, the camp was expensive with coaching, room, food, and expenses. But Uncle Martin had decided to pitch in and pay for the camp.

Quinn wasn't going to be happy. She'd been talking about going to Boston, the Cape, the beach, aquariums, science museums, and the list went on. "We need to do everything and have fun before the school year starts," she'd said.

I knew she was worried about going off to college or, more importantly, that she and I would not be going to the same college. It was a huge possibility. Her dream was to attend a medical school in North Carolina. Mine was to play basketball for UCLA or Ohio State. Yet if I didn't sharpen my court skills, then I wouldn't be going anywhere.

The music grew louder the closer we got to the barn.

"I'll tell her tonight." I had to. I was leaving in two days, and tomorrow I had to get my gear ready. "Jessica Bento, huh? I thought you swore off girls." He'd gotten his heart hurt when we'd moved to Massachusetts two years ago and he'd had to leave his last girlfriend behind.

"It's time for me to get back in the saddle, bro. You know, hormones and all."

I laughed. "The hand isn't cutting it anymore?"

He busted out laughing. "Not at all. Besides, have you seen Jessica's legs?"

Ethan and I preferred lithe, long legs rather than ogling girls' tits. "Can't say I have. She's a cheerleader, right? Pretty blonde?"

"A hot cheerleader, dude. And her legs go on forever, if you know what I mean."

"Please tell me you're using a condom," I said.

"Says my brother, who hasn't lost his virginity yet. Of course."

It was sad that my younger brother had lost his before me. "I told you—Quinn's not ready." We'd come close many times, but each time, she'd gotten cold feet. To be honest, I had too. I wished Dad were alive so we could talk about girls, sex, and life.

But thoughts of sex went out the window when Ethan and I approached the barn, which was bursting with kids. Many were dancing, several were holding red cups, and some were lingering around talking or watching others.

Quinn bounced out like she was high on life, her butterscotch hair flowing in silky waves behind her.

I lost the ability to speak as my gaze swept over my girl. Her sparkly low-cut tank top did a number on my libido. But her long, tanned legs were even more heart-throbbing.

Before I could say hi or come out of my lustful stupor, she grabbed my hand and tugged me out of the fray and around the side of the barn. When I inhaled her sweet berry shampoo, my brain went fuzzy, and my body reacted in a heated bliss.

All the talk about long legs, sex, and girls made me want to do things to Quinn I'd dreamed about at night or thought about in the shower. I'd even imagined doing those things as I kissed her endlessly. We were well aware of our sexual desire for one another, and if we didn't do something soon, I just might combust.

She pushed me against the barn, biting her lower lip.

"What are you doing?" My voice cracked.

Quinn was usually shy and wasn't aggressive at all when it came to taking advantage of me.

She giggled, pressing her gorgeous body against mine.

My arms went around her waist as though it were the most natural thing in the world. Then my hands roamed freely up and down her back, butt, and everywhere.

She moaned as she crashed her mouth to mine, her tongue begging for entrance.

Who was I to say no? But I detected a hint of alcohol on her. "Quinn?"

"Hush," she said in a breathy tone before her tongue snaked into my mouth.

"Have you been drinking?"

She peppered kisses along my neck. "A little."

"Whoa! Since when do you drink?"

Flattening her hands on my chest, she pushed and rolled her eyes. "I had two shots. We're seniors. It's time to let loose, Maiken. I'm not drunk. And I'm not about to do anything stupid. I'm not Marcus." She slurred most of the words.

I froze, not at the mention of my brother but because of her snippy attitude. I was finding that drunk people did and said stupid things.

She pouted. "I'm sorry. I didn't mean that."

"It's not about Marcus. I'm shocked you even tried liquor. What's gotten into you?" I had no idea if she was the same shy girl I'd met two years ago. Actually, that wasn't true. She wasn't. She had come out of her shell in the last year or so, and I hadn't complained until now.

She slipped her hand in between us and latched onto my belt. "Don't be a party pooper."

I arched a brow. "Me? You were the one worried about Marcus drinking."

She slid her hand down to my very hard erection. "Ooh. What's this?"

Every muscle in my body tensed.

Her big amber eyes popped. "You're hard." She squeezed my dick, a move she'd done a few times during our make-out sessions.

My eyes rolled back in my head. "Quinn."

"Hush." She proceeded to unbuckle my belt.

My brain said to stop her, but my body protested. "What are you doing?"

Her tongue darted out to wet her lips. Her attention was completely absorbed in unbuttoning my jeans.

Get her to stop. This isn't the place for sex. Plus, she's not herself.

She unzipped my jeans, and before I could take a breath, her small hand was inside my underwear.

Holy hell.

She started to crouch down.

"Quinn," my voice squeaked.

"Let me," she moaned, a sound that drove me insane.

Reluctantly, I grabbed her shoulders. "I want you more than anything, but not like this."

She continued to plow forward.

"Quinn," I said again. "Someone is going to see us." I was a terrible boyfriend for not pushing her harder to stop. All I could think about was her father catching us in the act.

She stroked.

Oh my word. "Quinn." My tone was more forceful, even though the feeling of her hand on me was out of this world, and something she hadn't been brave enough to do before.

I could hear a rustling of sorts somewhere nearby, and my stomach fell to the ground. "Your dad," I managed to say, even though I didn't want her to stop. But if she didn't, I was going to do something that would be extremely embarrassing.

I pictured our first time in other positions and in a quiet spot where no one was around. Not in the middle of a party with Carter nearby or a slew of high school kids who loved taking videos and pictures.

She flew back as if I'd lit a match to her skin. "Where?" Her head swiveled in all directions.

I rushed toward the darkness of the farm where no lights existed. I wasn't trying to run from her, but I needed to compose myself and make sure that whatever I'd heard wasn't her father lurking nearby. Then again, if it were him, he would definitely not lurk. He would pounce with an ax to my knees.

"Where are you going?" she called out.

"I need a minute. Go back to the party. I'll meet you inside."

She giggled. "I don't see my dad."

"What's going on?" Carter asked just as I disappeared into the darkness. "Who are you talking to?"

"I thought Daddy was out here," she said.

I kept walking across the farm, trying to get my heart to calm down and my libido under control.

And I thought I had to worry about Marcus.

Chapter 3

Quinn

Carter folded his arms over his chest as though he were some big, bad dude about to scare off a heard of boys. "Where's your boyfriend, sis?"

I loved my brother, but I didn't miss him ruining my life around boys. When Maiken and I first met, Carter had been a thorn in my side. He hated Maiken being near me.

Still, I couldn't let him smell the alcohol. That would be a huge disaster. "Maiken went up to his car to get something." *Liar, liar, pants on fire.*

Carter looked up at the parking lot. "I don't see him anywhere."

"Go back to Brianna." I hoped I wasn't slurring. The two shots had done a number on me. I was suddenly regretting succumbing to Celia's peer pressure, and Jack's too.

"Well, ladies, why don't you start this party by having a drink with me?" Jack had asked after setting up his equipment. "Alcohol gets me in a good mood to play music."

I'd been hesitant at first, but when I thought of Marcus and the potential disaster that might happen, I decided one drink wouldn't hurt. As soon as the liquor seeped into my veins, a warm feeling blanketed me, and suddenly I was buzzing. After the second shot, I hadn't cared about Marcus or anything. I felt energized, powerful, and brave.

"Sis." Carter's voice cut through my reverie. "Are you okay?"

Blinking, I focused on his hard features. "I'm fine. Stop playing Dad. I don't need you to babysit me. Either go back to sucking face with Brianna or leave."

He held up his hands, his amber eyes studying me like I was a lab specimen. "It seems you've changed drastically since I've been away at college."

He had no idea. Heat crawled up my neck and pinched my cheeks. If he knew what I had been doing a minute or two ago, he would literally shoot Maiken even though I was the hussy, a term my granny liked to use to define fast women who threw themselves at men. Yeah, I got the first-place award for that one tonight.

I giggled, thinking about Maiken's penis.

Carter arched a brow. "What's so funny?"

I'd forgotten he was standing a few feet away.

Lifting my chin, I lost my smile. "You," I lied. "Carter, I'm not a little girl anymore." *I am woman. Hear me roar.* "I don't need a big brother watching out for me."

Note to self: Maybe I should drink more alcohol.

His lips curled at the edges. "You're right."

I cocked my head. "I am?"

"I only came down with Brianna because Mom asked me to. But you're a senior. You should have a good time."

I figuratively scratched my head. "Are you my brother?"

He full-on laughed, a sound I hadn't heard from him in ages. Carter had always been a cranky teenager. "Quinn, I'm not home for the summer to babysit you. Actually, I don't want to be here. Brianna and I can be doing other things."

I could too if he hadn't interrupted Maiken and me.

He stabbed his thumb behind him. "I'm going to find Brianna. Have a good time." He strutted a way, running his hand through his short brown hair.

I didn't move for a moment, stymied by his words, and when he went into the barn, I scanned the area as far as I could see for Maiken or my dad.

Whoa! My dad. I shivered at the thought that he could've caught us.

Celia came running out of the barn like a tornado on steroids, looking like she'd stolen the red cup in her hand. "Quinn, I've been looking all over for you. The party is rocking." Then she slyly glanced around before thrusting the cup at me. "Here."

I took the cup, sniffing as the aroma of alcohol floated out. "There's enough liquor in here to burn my nose hairs."

She giggled then snorted. "So drink. I added a bit of soda to cut it some."

I shook my head. "I can't. If I have any more, and I might make a bigger fool of myself." *Or scare Maiken away for good. Oh, and puke.*

She jutted out her chin, her defiant stance daring me not to drink. "You promised."

I puffed out my cheeks. I wasn't one to break my promises. "One more." With my luck, I would probably make a jerk out of myself. Oh wait, I already had with Maiken. "To our senior year." I lifted up the cup and chugged like an expert drinker.

Celia watched me, grinning.

I scrunched my nose, holding my breath as I drank the burning fluid. I swore if someone lit a match right then, I would burst into flames.

When I was done, I shivered violently. I knew then that I would pay dearly for this little stunt later.

"Good girl." Then she giggled and snorted. "Let's dance."

"I should go find Maiken."

"He's inside," she said. "He's talking to Liam by the food table."

He must've backtracked and gone into the barn on the other side.

She hooked her arm in mine as we walked inside. "I love this song."

"Teeth" by 5 Seconds of Summer was blaring from the speakers while bodies bounced up and down, dancing to their hearts' content.

Dizziness encroached as I searched for Maiken among the hundred or more heads. Yeah, forty had turned into fifty, then sixty, and so on. Daddy hadn't been down to break it up yet. But I figured he would at some point with how many kids were packed into the barn like sardines. At least there hadn't been any outbursts of tempers or fists flying, which was a good thing.

Suddenly, the music stopped.

Kids protested.

In the distance, Jack, who was up on a platform, set his headphones on a table and began examining why the music had died. "Sorry, folks," he said into the microphone. "Just a minor difficulty."

I wiped the sweat off my brow with my hand, listing to one side as I searched for Maiken. I really shouldn't have had that last drink.

"Fuck off," someone to my right screamed in a high-pitched voice.

The hairs on my arm stood upright as Celia and I exchanged a wide-eyed look.

I knew that voice. I zeroed in on—of all people—Sloane Price. *What is she doing at my party?* I didn't invite her.

As if Celia knew what I was thinking, she said, "Marcus."

Growling, I pushed through the crowd. People had no problem carving a path for me like I was the queen at this party.

Sloane, with her short white hair and big brown eyes, was facing off against Holly Camara. Holly was the same height as Sloane, with long brown hair and blue eyes. Where Sloane had the weight, Holly had the muscle. The girl was in shape since she danced and did cheer-leading.

"I was talking to Marcus." Holly snarled at Sloane. "He's not yours anymore."

I grabbed Sloane's arm and spun her to face me. "I didn't invite you."

She'd broken up with Marcus recently and was moving out of town.

Marcus stood behind the girls, watching intently with a smug grin as though he were enjoying being the proud peacock.

Sloane twisted her pink-painted lips, pinning her brown gaze on me. "Marcus invited me."

I sneered at the younger Maxwell brother. "He was invited out of pity."

Marcus didn't react, which only infuriated me more.

Tessa Stevens, my former archenemy and head cheerleader, came to her teammate's rescue. "Holly, she's not worth it. She's moving anyways. Marcus will be free soon."

Holly shrugged off Tessa, wanting nothing more than to deck Sloane.

Oh, hell no.

"This is my party," I said to Sloane. "Marcus had no right to invite you. So leave now."

Sloane's nostrils flared as she got in my face, practically touching my nose with hers "Or what, Quinn? You're too much of a coward to punch me."

She did not just say that. I didn't even think. My fist was flying in one second flat. The crack of my knuckles hitting her jaw sounded like joy and felt like agony as the pain zipped up my arm.

As if my punch were the gun that went off to start a road race, shouts and catcalls ensued.

"Fight. Fight. Fight," the crowd chanted.

Sloane returned the gesture, only she hit my mouth and not my nose.

Stars danced in my vision as blood seeped into my mouth. The metallic taste burst on my tongue and woke me up.

But before I could react, Celia jumped on Sloane's back and grabbed handfuls of my enemy's hair. "You can't hit my best friend."

"Get off me," Sloane shrieked, throwing Celia to the ground.

As if in slow motion, my BFF fell backward, her head colliding with the barn floor.

Holly dove at Sloane, who fell into me, and I went down hard on my butt.

Liam ran up. "Ladies, enough!"

Maiken emerged from the crowd. "Quinn, are you okay?"

I crawled over to Celia on my hands and knees. Any pain I had was muted when I saw her unconscious. "Celia!" I tapped on her face, but she didn't move. "Celia? Celia?" Tears burned my eyes, acid scorched my throat, and I had the urge to throw up.

Liam joined me on the floor, feeling for a pulse. "Maiken, call an ambulance. Dustin, get my dad. He's up at the house."

Tears poured out as I tapped Celia's face again. "Hey, wake up."

Hands landed on the sides of my arms. "Quinn," Marcus said.

I popped to my feet. This was all his fault. He'd invited Sloane. He attracted trouble. I reached out to push him, but I listed to one side, and my knees buckled.

Maiken, who was on my other side, caught me. "I got her, bro." He ushered me outside, passing the watching and judging eyes. Some people even had their phones out, recording what was happening.

Great. Not the way I wanted my party to be remembered.

"Does she have a pulse?" I managed to say before I ran to the edge of the barn. I didn't have a chance to bend over before the puke came out in a projectile stream. My head spun like I was on a fast-moving merry-go-round.

Maiken rubbed my back. "Let it all out."

"Go away, please." The words stammered out before I puked again.

"Party is over," Daddy's voice roared. He sounded like a lion about to attack.

I was in deep trouble.

Chapter 4

Maiken

Quinn puked her guts out, and the scent of alcohol flowed in my direction.

Mr. Thompson was wrangling kids out of the barn. "Carter, go up to the top of the back driveway and guide the ambulance down here."

Mrs. Thompson ran down, her head turning in every direction. "Quinn?"

I waved at Mrs. Thompson. "Over here."

Quinn's mom dodged the kids leaving and rushed to Quinn's side. "You've been drinking?" Her tone was full of disappointment and shock.

I hated to think how much trouble Quinn was going to be in with her parents. I was sure Mr. Thompson, who was quite scary, would ground her for the rest of the year.

Mrs. Thompson pinned me with a stern expression. "Maiken, have you been drinking too?"

Quinn puked again.

"No, ma'am." After seeing what liquor had done to Marcus, I wasn't rushing out to try the stuff. Actually, Dad had let me taste a few sips of his beer once, and I didn't see what the fuss was all about.

"I'll take care of Quinn. Go help Jeff and my boys."

I regarded my girlfriend, who had her back to me. "Quinn?" I didn't want to leave her. Then again, I couldn't do much anyway.

"Do what my mom says." Quinn's tone was rough and scratchy.

Mrs. Thompson flicked her head, her brown hair falling out of her bun. "She'll be fine."

I doubted she would, at least not for a while. Nevertheless, I plowed through the kids who were lingering outside the barn. The paramedics were lifting Celia onto a stretcher. Liam was close by, biting his nails. I'd learned earlier that he and Celia had broken up, but from the panic in his eyes, he still cared for her.

Ethan was standing next to Marcus, who had his arm around Sloane. I guessed she'd won Marcus's attention since I didn't see Holly anywhere.

I had the urge to give Sloane a piece of my mind, but it wouldn't do any good. Sloane and Marcus were on a different planet than the rest of us. They walked to a beat of their own, and frankly, I was tired of trying to get through to my brother.

Marcus said something in Sloane's ear. Then the two slipped through the crowd and made their way out.

Ethan came up to me. "That went well. You want to stop him from leaving?"

"Nope. Let him do whatever it is he's going to do." Marcus was the least of my worries. I tossed a look over my shoulder, but I couldn't see Quinn from where I was standing just inside the barn. I didn't even see her walking up to the house.

"You say that all the time but then get in his face."

A group of kids were lingering and watching as Mr. Thompson talked to the paramedics.

"He didn't start the fight." My girl kind of had, which was mind-blowing. Then again, she was under the influence of alcohol. If she hadn't been, she wouldn't have outright punched Sloane.

What is it about drinking? I didn't get the eagerness to try beer or vodka or whatever. Still, my senior year wasn't going to revolve around babysitting Marcus. I'd done that last year, and the aftereffects had landed me in the hospital. I wasn't repeating that again. As much as I loved Quinn, I wasn't her babysitter either.

My senior year would be focused on basketball, scouts, college scholarships, and spending as much time with Quinn as I could before we both went our separate ways next year. At least I expected we would go to different colleges since her plan was medical school and mine was basketball.

The paramedics carried Celia away with Liam following closely.

Mr. Thompson ran a hand through his brown hair, appearing angry, tired, and ready to yell at someone.

Carter, who I just noticed standing not far from his dad, narrowed his gaze on me before stalking over.

Here we go.

Carter wagged his finger. "This is your fault."

Ethan slid his hand in between Carter and me. "Back off, dude. My brother had nothing to do with any of this."

Carter ignored Ethan as though he weren't standing next to me. "You got my sister drunk so you could take advantage of her. She was with you around the barn earlier. Wasn't she?"

I put a hand on my brother's arm. "Ethan, I can handle Carter."

Ethan lowered his hand but didn't leave.

I inched closer to Carter. "I don't control your sister's actions." Then I blew in his face. "Do you smell alcohol on me? No. So fuck off." The last thing I wanted to do was fight him or cause any more trouble. But I wasn't about to let him pin any of the evening's events on me.

Carter's nostrils flared. "If I find out you had anything to do with this, I will end you once and for all."

I stuck out my chin. "Dude, go back to college. Stay out of our business." Then I sauntered away, not giving him a second look. "Ethan, let's go to the hospital." Carter hated me, but Liam didn't, and since he and I were good friends, I wanted to support him.

Ethan brushed his shoulder against Carter's as he passed by.

Carter caught his arm. "You Maxwells are all alike. You think your shit doesn't stink. You think you own this town. Your cousins were the same way."

Ethan stood toe to toe with Carter, almost eye to eye. "You sound jealous, dude. And next time you feel the need to threaten my brother, think twice. Because you'll have more than one of us to deal with."

Carter plastered on an evil grin. "Bring it, dude."

I gripped Ethan's shoulder. "Not here, man. People are watching too."

Quinn ran down the path from the house.

Her mother stood on the deck with her hands on her hips. "Quinn," she shouted.

Carter pushed Ethan's shoulder as he rushed to block Quinn. "Mom is calling you."

Quinn shoved him out of the way, or she tried. "I want to see Celia. I'm going with her to the hospital."

The lights of the ambulance were fading as they left the farm.

Carter gripped her arms. "Liam is going with her. Go up to the house and get cleaned up. You look a mess."

Quinn glared at her older brother. "Fuck you."

I felt like I was in an alternate universe, not exactly sure who Quinn was right now. I knew what alcohol did to a person. Hell, Marcus had given us a front-row seat to his drunken behavior a few times already, and I didn't like the drunk Quinn. If her idea of letting loose was to take up drinking or anything else, like drugs, then our relationship was in jeopardy.

"We need to get out of here." Ethan's voice broke through my trance.

I kicked my legs into gear alongside Ethan, and we headed up to the lot by the farm store.

"Maiken," Mr. Thompson called.

I briefly closed my eyes. If I ignored him, he would tear into me, and the last thing I wanted to do was make my girlfriend's dad madder than he already was. Not only that, I respected my elders.

I pivoted on my heel, coming face-to-face with a Carter lookalike.

Mr. Thompson's signature scowl was ever present. That glower had terrified me many times when I'd first met him. "Have you been drinking? Is that why my daughter is drunk?"

I swallowed my own anger, which was primed to lash out. *Why does everyone think I forced Quinn to drink?* Then again, like father, like son.

"No, sir," I said in a polite tone, even though it was difficult not to shout at him.

He glared, studying me.

"Sir, we haven't been drinking," Ethan said at my side.

Quinn cried nearby. "I hate you," she said to Carter, or maybe she was talking to her mom.

The wrinkles around Mr. Thompson's eyes relaxed. "Go home."

Ethan and I didn't waste any time in getting the hell out of there.

Quinn was in a world of shit, and I doubted I would see her any time soon.

"Maiken," Mr. Thompson said. "You're not allowed to see my daughter until further notice."

Well, there went my goal of spending time with my girl, which probably wouldn't matter anyway, at least not for the next four weeks. I was off to basketball camp for most of the summer. Maybe when I got back, this night would be a distant memory, and Quinn and I could pick up where we'd left off.

Yet somehow, I didn't think things between us would ever be normal again.

Chapter 5

Quinn

I trudged up to the house, stomping my feet as I passed Momma. I couldn't remember the last time I'd acted like I was five years old when I didn't get my way.

"Quinn, get cleaned up. Your father and I will be in to talk to you shortly," Momma tossed out over her shoulder.

Tears streamed down my cheeks as the blood on my lip began to dry. I should be scared about what punishment Momma and Daddy would dole out, but I didn't care. I cared about Celia. She wasn't conscious, and I needed to see her.

I stopped at the sliding glass door. "Mom, I want to see Celia."

"No!" Her tone was frightening, and it had been years since she snapped at me. "You'll be lucky if you leave this house for the next six months."

I dashed away tears, opened the door, and trudged inside as my heart splintered and shattered. It was all my fault that Celia had gotten hurt.

Damn Sloane and Marcus. I blamed Marcus more. I knew I shouldn't have let him come to the party.

I sobbed as I climbed the stairs.

Stupid. Stupid. Stupid.

My head pounded as though someone had taken a sledgehammer to it, and my stomach swirled like an out-of-control tornado.

I rushed into the bathroom and barely made it to the toilet. After emptying my stomach again, I grabbed some toilet paper and wiped my mouth. Then I went over to the mirror and gasped. My upper lip was swollen. My hair stuck out in every direction. My skin was as white as snow, and my eyes were bloodshot. Plus, my mouth was dry and parched.

I splashed water on my face, hoping it would clear my senses or at least get the color to return. After drying off, I fumbled for my phone in the back pocket of my shorts. Then I called Liam.

The phone rang until his voice mail picked up. "Liam, please call me. I need to know that Celia's okay."

I sighed and then broke down in more tears. Maybe Maiken was on his way to the hospital. I called him, but his voice mail answered too.

"Hey, can you call me?"

I slumped against the sink when my phone pinged.

Maiken: *We'll talk tomorrow.*

My mind spun. What the heck did he mean we would talk tomorrow?

Me: *I want to talk now. Are you going to the hospital?*

Maiken: *Liam called me and told me not to.*

Me: *Please go. I have to make sure Celia's okay.*

Maiken: *Liam will give us an update.*

Me: *I'm sorry about tonight.*

He had to think I was a freak. He hated when Marcus drank, and now his girlfriend was falling into the same dark hole as his brother.

Maiken: *Get some rest.*

Me: *I'm sure I'm grounded.*

Maiken: *Yep.*

Me: *I'll come over tomorrow when I take Apple for a ride.*

Maiken: *I won't be around.*

Me: *Where are you going?*

My heart plummeted. Surely one mishap on my part wasn't cause for not seeing me.

Maiken: *My mom is taking me shopping.*

I sighed.

Me: *Call me afterwards, then?*

Maiken: *Sure.*

Me: *I love you.*

I fixated on the bright screen, waiting for a response, but none came.

Me: *Are you still there?*

My heart punched my ribs like I'd punched Sloane, and it hurt.

After a few minutes with no response, I called Maiken again. The line rang and rang and rang until his voice mail connected.

I hiccupped and hung up. I was too much of a hot mess to leave a message. He hated me. I was sure of it.

I checked my text messages again, but there was still no response. I tried one more time to get him on the phone. Again, he didn't answer.

Tears poured out of my bloodshot eyes. I'd ruined everything, including my party and my chances of having any more parties. I might have lost my boyfriend, and my BFF had been rushed to the hospital.

Sobbing, I slid down the counter until my butt was on the floor. Then I brought my knees to my chest and buried my head in my hands.

Footsteps pounded outside the bathroom door. "Quinn," Carter said before he knocked.

"Go away," I cried.

"Dad wants you downstairs in ten minutes." Carter's tone made me shiver. He had a lot of the same qualities as our dad—deep voice, commanding presence, and strict in his morals when it came to what girls should and should not do. However, the one difference was that Carter didn't give an inch. At least I could reason with Daddy. With Carter, there was no reasoning. I pitied his future daughters.

Regardless, I didn't think any amount of reasoning with Daddy was going to work that night.

Take your licks and keep your mouth shut. Daddy might be lenient.

I would like to believe the voice in my head, but I knew I was in a world of shit.

I hardly had time for a shower, but I couldn't go downstairs looking like I'd been dragged through pig shit and mud. So I jumped in the shower and rinsed off, although no amount of water would wash away what I'd done. Fifteen minutes later, I wound my way downstairs.

Momma's voice trickled out of the kitchen. "Call when you have news. Oh, and Liam, give my best to her mom."

I padded lightly down the hall until I was standing in the arched doorway between the kitchen and family room.

Daddy was sitting at our picnic-style table, drinking from a coffee cup. "How's Celia?"

I slid off to the side so he wouldn't see me.

"Not good," Momma said.

I covered my mouth with my hand to stop the sob that was about to come barreling out.

"Liam will keep us posted." Momma's voice was filled with sadness.

"Quinn, I know you're listening. Get in here now!" Daddy's voice boomed.

I shivered as if I were standing naked outside in the dead of winter. I took one tiny step at a time and inched into the brightly lit kitchen. It blinded me, yet darkness encroached from all sides as I settled near the fridge, away from Daddy.

His brown gaze was soaking in fury. The wrinkles on his forehead were deep, and his nostrils were opening and closing like he was struggling for air.

I swallowed a lump of coal as I regarded Momma. Her lips were pursed, her features tight, and her gaze as hard as stone.

The silence was maddening, and the longer neither of them said anything, the more my insides spun. I didn't think I had anything else to throw up, but my stomach was telling me otherwise.

I flipped my wet hair over my shoulder for nothing else than to expel some nerves.

Daddy finally spoke. "What do you have to say for yourself?"

The last time I had done anything to warrant Daddy's wrath had been in the eighth grade. He'd warned me not to go near a new horse we'd had at the time.

"I need to break him before you ride him," Daddy had said. "It's dangerous. Do you understand?"

"But I can break him," I'd returned.

"Absolutely not. He'll kill you."

I hadn't listened to him. I'd wanted to show him I could break in the horse. However, the minute I took the horse out of the stall, he'd gotten spooked at a loud noise in the barn. I'd ended up with bruised ribs and an ego to match. Daddy had been irritated and scared that day, not glaringly furious.

"I'm waiting, young lady."

Momma watched, her expression unwavering.

I locked my trembling fingers together in front of me. "I'm sorry." That was all I could say. I had no other words.

"Where did you get the liquor?" Momma asked.

I bit my lip. "Some boy."

"Name." Daddy's tone was hard and scary.

I couldn't throw Jack under the bus. "A lot of kids had liquor. I don't remember."

Daddy let out a long breath as if trying to control his temper. "Someone told me that you threw the first punch. Is that true?"

Slowly, I nodded as I stared at my orange-painted toenails. It was useless to rehash what had happened. The damage was done. Someone had gotten hurt. I'd started the fight. I'd gotten tipsy. I'd ruined my party. It was no one's fault but mine.

I inhaled deeply. "Just tell me my punishment."

Daddy slapped a hand down on the table. The sound exploded as if a bomb had gone off. "Don't take that tone with me. Let's go back to last year when you and I had a conversation outside church the day after the party where the Maxwell boy was passed out drunk and bleeding. Do you remember what you told me?"

It was hard to forget Sloane's party. Maiken had had to carry a drunken Marcus out. But as I dipped back to that Sunday, my heart stopped.

"I don't want you going to anymore parties," Daddy said.

"Why?

"Quinn, parties only attract trouble. I don't want to see you get caught up with the wrong crowd either."

"You can't shelter me forever, Daddy."

"I'm doing this for your own good."

Daddy cleared his throat. "What did you tell me that day? I want to hear you say it."

I blinked. "I told you to trust me. I said I wouldn't drink or try drugs."

"What else?" He didn't forget a thing.

"You and Mom taught me responsibility."

Momma was sipping her coffee, resting against the counter, and watching me like a hawk. "Where was your responsibility tonight?"

I swallowed hard. I'd promised both of them I would never drink or do drugs.

"We allowed you to have this party because we trusted you, Quinn," Momma said. "We also told you to limit the party to fifty. There were close to a hundred kids in that barn."

Again, I couldn't give her an excuse or tell her truthfully how the party had gotten so out of hand. I also shouldn't have been surprised. By inviting one person, I might as well have invited the whole damn school. The news of a party always spread like wildfire.

But in all fairness to me, it was summer, which meant families left town on vacations.

"You broke our trust, Quinn." The disappointment in Daddy's tone made my stomach clench far worse than his anger.

"I'm sorry." It was all I could say. "It will never happen again."

Daddy rose and pushed his fingers through his short brown hair. "Darn right it won't. You're grounded for the summer. No parties. No friends. And that means Maiken too. You'll pull extra shifts on the farm and in the store."

"But Daddy," I cried. "I want to see Celia."

Daddy regarded Momma.

"We'll wait to hear from Liam," Momma said. "Until then, go up to your room."

I hesitated, but Momma gave me one of those "I dare you to beg" looks, so I ran out.

I started to climb the stairs then stopped when I heard Daddy's voice.

"I pray no one left this party drunk and decided to drive."

"Jeff, honey, take a breath," Momma said. "Your blood pressure is high enough as it is."

"I expected something like this from the boys, but not Quinn," he said in defeat.

Heavy footfalls made me flinch, and I turned my attention to the top of the stairs as Carter came down.

"Eavesdropping, Quinn?"

I threw him the finger, ready to lock myself in my room until next summer.

"Come with me," he said.

"I can't. I'm supposed to be in my room."

Carter peered around the bannister. "They won't know."

I arched a brow and shook my head. "Yes, they will."

"I'll take the blame," he said.

I didn't want to be alone, and I wouldn't be able to sleep until I knew Celia was going to be okay.

I huffed. "Fine. If Daddy doubles my punishment, I'll make sure Brianna knows the real you."

He chuckled as he flicked his head to the front door. "Let's go."

I debated for a second before I followed Carter out the door and onto the porch. "Where are we going?"

"Do you want to see Celia or not?"

I glanced at my jersey-fabric shorts and T-shirt.

Carter angled his head. "You look fine."

If I went back inside, I wouldn't get a chance to see Celia. At least I was wearing a bra, and I did have on flip-flops.

Carter's gaze drifted past me. "Your window is closing, sis."

I didn't know why he was doing this for me. Daddy would lay into him as hard as he had me.

I sighed heavily. I might be banging another nail into my coffin, but I had to be there for Celia. If the tables were turned, she would jump through hell to be there for me.

I ran down the porch steps and climbed into his truck. I would take whatever additional punishment Daddy handed down.

Chapter 6

Maiken

Mom had her laptop on her legs, glasses perched on her nose, and a cup of coffee in her hands as she read something on her computer screen.

I stepped down off the last step and onto our worn wooden floor. "You're up early for a Sunday."

The only room Mom had not renovated in our new farmhouse was the family room. It was the one area where we spent the most time, and she didn't see any reason to put money into new floors or furniture, since we were kids who had accidents and played rough.

"Too hot to sleep," she said, not glancing up from her screen. "I should be saying the same to you. You kids never get up before nine, and it's only seven thirty."

I wound my way around one of two couches and a chair then dropped down next to her. "I thought the summers in North Carolina and Texas were brutal." I yawned.

She tapped a key on her computer. "We had air-conditioned homes when we lived there. It's too expensive to have the house outfitted for it here. Besides, I want to put my money into a new heating system before winter sets in. The fireplace in this room only heats up this area."

I eyed the stone fireplace, which was tall enough for my younger sisters and brothers to walk into. Mom had used it quite a bit last winter right after we'd moved in.

I rubbed the sleep out of my eyes, squinting at the rays of sun spilling in through one of three windows facing the front yard.

My mind drifted to the night before as I listened to Mom's fingers fly over her keyboard.

What a mess the party had been. Quinn had kept texting me and calling me, but I'd wanted her to sleep it off before we talked. Nothing good would've come from our conversation while she was under the influence.

"Mom, when you were a teenager, did you ever get drunk?"

Her fingers froze over the keyboard. "Was Marcus drinking last night?"

"No." Although he might have been after he left the party, but I didn't want to plant any seeds for her to get freaked out over. Besides, Marcus was asleep in his room. I'd checked when I passed his room earlier. "Quinn was tipsy. Well, more than tipsy." I blew out a heavy breath as our quiet interlude flashed before me.

Stop thinking about that. You're sitting next to your mom.

"Is that why you kids came home early? I asked Emma, but she didn't elaborate. She just said a fight broke out, and Marcus wasn't part of it. Then she got a phone call, as I was putting Harlan to bed."

I popped my head back against the couch. "Quinn started the fight."

She wiped her brow with her fingers, moving wisps of her dirty-blond hair from her forehead. "Is that so? Jeff and Hazel must be beside themselves."

"Oh yeah. Mr. Thompson was furious. I'm not allowed to see Quinn until further notice." Knowing her dad, Quinn was probably grounded for the rest of her high school days.

"So, Emma didn't mention that Celia was rushed to the hospital?"

My mom gasped. "Oh God, no! Is Celia okay?"

I shrugged. "I think so." I hadn't heard from Liam, but no news was good news... usually. "I need to call Liam."

"Was Celia drinking too?" Mom asked.

I bobbed my head.

Her tone dropped. "And you and Ethan?"

"No, ma'am."

She sighed before taking a swig of coffee as though caffeine was her alcohol. "Look, son. It doesn't matter if I drank in high school. What matters is knowing the effects of what alcohol and drugs can do to a person. It's important to never get behind the wheel impaired and use alcohol or drugs as a crutch to drown your problems."

I kicked up my legs and rested my bare feet on the coffee table, which was littered with pamphlets and folders.

Leaning forward, I picked up a pamphlet. "Are you sending us to Greenridge Academy?" *Please say no, at least not me.* "Is this the school that the triplets went to?"

She frowned as she brought her cup up to her lips. "I'm thinking about it. You boys need structure. I would like to say I can handle the eight of you, and I actually think I did a pretty good job when your dad was on deployment. But I didn't have five teenagers to discipline."

I flipped through the pamphlet, perusing the pictures of happy students holding books, an aerial view of the school, the football field, and even the gymnasium. I swallowed thickly as my stomach sank. "You're sending me too?" I held my breath.

She studied me while she drank her coffee.

I stopped on the last page of the pamphlet. "Is this…"

"Yep," she said. "That's Kross."

My cousin Kross Maxwell was in a boxing ring, sparring with an older man.

"I think Marcus and Jasper will like the school," Mom said. "Marcus likes boxing, and Jasper loves any sport. You know, they have a great basketball program. Lots of their students go on to great colleges and universities, and I've been told scouts love what they see from the students. Many of them, according to the brochures, have been drafted into the NBA and NFL and other major sports organizations, even the Olympics."

It sounded like she was trying to convince herself more than me. I fixated on a younger version of Kross, and even as a teenager, he was built much like Marcus. I also didn't doubt that what the brochure touted was true. I just didn't want to leave home or start over.

My mom sat back in her chair. "I'm going up to visit the school before I make a decision. I know you'll be at camp, but the rest of the family is going with me. Kross is even coming to show us around. He knows several of the staff. He's been in touch with the boxing coach the last few years as well."

"So no firm decision?" I didn't want to argue with her. She'd been through enough with everything that had happened in our family since Dad passed away. Maybe she would decide in the end not to ship off her boys. "What about Emma? Is she included?"

Mom set her cup down on the table. Then she laid her hand on my leg. "I don't like what I might have to do, Maiken. I want your support if I decide to flip the switch."

I lowered the brochure to my lap. "I don't want to go. I'm sure it's a good school. But I just got into the groove at Kensington. My back is better, which means I can play better, and I want to take the team to state. If I go to a new school, I'll be the black sheep again. And it's my senior year, Mom."

Her brown eyes were soft as she considered me. "Tell you what. We'll talk more when you get back from camp. I'll have weighed the pros and cons for each of you, and yes, Emma will be included. Actually, she's the most excited. They have a great volleyball team, and some of the girls have gone on to play in the Olympics."

She'd warned us last year when she'd talked with Emma, Ethan, Marcus, and me. I remembered her exact words.

"I understand that your father's passing has been difficult. But drinking isn't the way to cope. Fighting isn't either. I'm sorry I haven't been there for all of you, but if things don't change, then maybe military school will give you the structure you need."

Regardless, the summer was starting out with a hell of a bang. Marcus had been a pain since school let out, or rather since Sloane had broken up with him, causing Mom to contemplate some difficult decisions.

My girl was a different person all of a sudden. Yet it had just been one incident, so I couldn't give up on her. I loved her too much to let one bad decision ruin our relationship.

My focus, though, was basketball. It had to be. The sport was my ticket to college—at least I was praying it was—so whether I played at Kensington or another school, then so be it.

Chapter 7

Quinn

I hugged my knees to my chest as I rocked in a hard chair in a small, windowless waiting room at the hospital. It felt like I was in jail, and the four bare walls were closing in on me.

My head pounded like there was a small person inside banging a hammer against my skull. My mouth was bone dry, and my stomach kept growling. At least I wasn't puking.

So this is what a hangover feels like. I didn't think I'd had that much to drink, but I guessed I had.

Carter strutted in like he'd gotten a good night's sleep. His amber eyes were bright, his brown hair was combed back, and he held two cups with lids in his hands. He gave me one. "Drink."

I needed something to take away the nastiness in my mouth. "What is it?" It wasn't hot.

He dropped down in the chair next to me. "Tomato juice. It will help."

"You know this from experience?" He probably did. After all, he was in college, and I was sure he went to frat parties.

"It doesn't matter. Mom called. She wants you to come home."

I sipped the juice, scrunching up my nose. The acidity was pungent. "I'll probably be grounded longer now."

He sipped on his beverage, which smelled like coffee. "She's not happy with either one of us."

"Why did you bring me anyway?" I hadn't asked him yet.

On the car ride over last night, my brain had been foggy, and I hadn't exactly been in a talking mood. I doubted he would've fessed up either. Carter didn't like talking unless he was yelling at someone, although since he'd gotten home from college for the summer, he seemed different. It was as though he was seeing the world from a different perspective, or maybe he really had grown wings and flown the coop.

He lifted his broad shoulders. "You were going to find a way on your own. So I wanted to make it easier for you and soften the blow with Mom and Dad."

"Who are you, and what did you do with my brother?" I teased.

"What's that supposed to mean?" He sounded hurt.

I took another drink of the nasty juice. "You're not exactly one to help me break the rules."

"Can't I help my sister?"

I could probe more, but Carter was a closed-door kind of guy. He didn't show his feelings, nor would he tell me his secrets.

We sat in silence, both watching the door. I was waiting for Liam to return. He'd gone to see if he could find out more on Celia. So far, we'd learned she had a severe concussion. She also had a high level of alcohol in her system. The doctor was running tests to make sure she didn't have any bleeding in the brain. And she'd been in and out of consciousness.

"Why did you hit that girl?" Carter asked.

I licked the cut on my lip. "Wherever Sloane goes, trouble follows. I hated that she was there. I hated that she was ruining my party. In truth, I had some excess bad mojo with her, and the booze made me brave." I went on to explain what Sloane had done to Maiken last year.

"He's lucky he didn't get seriously hurt," Carter said as though he genuinely cared. "What was she doing at the party?"

"Marcus must've invited her, but I was surprised she even came. She just broke up with him." I couldn't keep up with their tense relationship. Toward the end of the school year, they had become two hellions. Marcus had started drinking again. Sloane had snubbed

Maiken and me in the halls at school, which was mind-blowing considering she'd broken down and told us about how her dad had died in a barn fire and how she blamed herself. Not only that, she'd been apologetic for her role in ruining Maiken's basketball season. She was an enigma for sure. "I was worried about Marcus doing something stupid at my party." I laughed. "I ended up doing the stupid thing. Now look. Celia got hurt because of me."

"I'm sorry about Celia. She's lucky, though."

I sighed. "No shit."

"You know us Thompsons have fire in our blood. It's about time you finally showed some of that," he said teasingly.

I smiled at Carter. I liked this softer side of my brother. I couldn't remember the last time he'd been so nice to me. It wasn't as if he treated me like crap, but he could be cold at times.

"It wasn't my first time throwing a punch. I hit her right after Maiken was rushed to the hospital last year."

He regarded me proudly. "For real?"

"It felt good to hit her. Well, not for my hand." I set the cup of juice down on the table next to me. I couldn't drink any more. "Are you in trouble with Mom and Dad for bringing me here?"

"What are they going to do to me? Dad could try and ground me, but I'm not a kid anymore. I have worse problems anyway."

My eyes widened. "What does that mean?"

He gave me a sidelong glance. "The week before the semester ended, I got arrested for being drunk and disorderly on campus."

I gasped, and the intake of air got stuck in my throat. Carter had always been the good boy. If he'd done something terrible in high school, he hadn't gotten caught. "Does Daddy know?"

He choked. "God no. If he did, he'd probably lock me up in the barn."

I giggled.

"What's so funny?"

I snorted. "Drunk, huh? Is there a pattern forming in our family?"

He grinned for a mere second before losing his smile. "I was lucky,

Quinn. One, I wasn't driving. Two, the dude I decked isn't pressing charges."

I bit a nail. "Do you think Sloane will press charges?" I hadn't even thought of that. I could go to jail. *No. No. No.*

He grabbed my hand from my mouth. "She won't."

My stomach churned. "You don't know that."

"Even if she does, nothing will come of it. She was out of control too."

I furrowed my brows. "Why is your situation different? I mean, why can the guy you hit press charges?"

He got up and dumped his cup into the trash near the door. "Because he was an innocent bystander at a party who looked at me the wrong way. Quinn, I prefer if Mom and Dad don't know."

Daddy would have a stroke if he knew Carter had been arrested. "I'm not a tattler." I yawned. My body was beginning to feel weak and tired.

My brother returned to his seat, his expression somber. "I know. Can I tell you something else in confidence?"

Carter and I had never ever told each other our secrets. "Of course."

"I'm thinking of dropping out of college."

What is happening around me? I felt as though the party had been some sort of launch to another planet. "Why?" I shouldn't have been surprised. Carter had never been into school. "You were the one who decided to go." Momma and Daddy hadn't forced him or encouraged him. Our parents might be strict, but they wanted us to make our own decisions when it came to college.

Liam ambled in. Black circles painted his tired amber eyes as he yawned. "I'm ready for bed."

I jumped up. "Celia?"

He sat down on the chair next to Carter. "Doc said she has no bleeding in her brain. She might not remember anything."

I bounced on my feet. "Is she talking? Awake? Can I see her?"

"Yeah. Her mom said to go in. She had to run home and get Celia some things. She'll be in for a few days. They want to watch her closely since her concussion is bad."

I bolted out the door and ran right into someone. It took me a second to get my bearings, and when I did, I cried, "Maiken!" I threw myself at him. "How come you didn't call me back or answer any more of my texts?" I sounded like a crazy teenager with off-the-chart hormones.

He gave me one of his slow, easy grins as his blue gaze drank me in.

Holy moly! I had to look like death. Then I remembered I was wearing my sleep shorts and matching T-shirt with llamas on them. My hair probably looked like I'd been in an F5 tornado. And hygiene? *Yikes!* Even though I'd taken a quick shower last night, I hadn't brushed my teeth yet. And my upper lip was swollen like I'd gotten a heavy dose of Botox.

I edged away, like far away. "I'm going to see Celia. Will you be here for a while?"

He peeked into the waiting room. "Can we talk outside?"

The hallway spun. "Sure. I guess. It can't wait?" I got the feeling he'd been ignoring me after I'd sent my fifty texts. Okay, so I hadn't really sent fifty, but any more than three was bordering on madness. Still, I got a sinking feeling that he was going to break up with me because of last night.

A pensive expression washed over him. "Sorry, it can't."

I folded my arms over my chest, feeling small and embarrassed.

Liam came out of the room. "Are you ready to leave tomorrow?"

"Leave?" The mouth dryness I'd had earlier returned, and I swallowed to get the lump in my throat to go down.

Did his mom decide to move again?

"Sorry, man," Liam said. "I thought you told Quinn already."

Maiken paled. "No worries."

Liam went back into the waiting room.

I bit my bottom lip. "What's he talking about?" I craned my neck up at my boyfriend, or maybe he would be my ex in the next minute or so.

Maybe moving was in the Ashford water.

"Are you feeling better?" Maiken asked.

I hugged myself. I had, but I wasn't anymore. "Tell me." I ground my back teeth together. Tears were on the precipice of spilling over like Niagara Falls.

Don't cry. You don't know what he's going to say yet.

He was leaving. That was crying material for me.

"I was going to tell you last night. Then the shit hit the fan. Anyway, I'm off to basketball camp for a month."

I should have been relieved it was just camp, but in my belly, I felt like a string in our relationship had broken. Maybe it was my hangover making me think the worst.

"You'll be gone the rest of the summer?"

He tucked his hands into his jeans pockets. "Pretty much. Didn't your dad ground you?"

Tears stung my eyes. I wasn't going to cry, at least not in front of Maiken.

"When did you decide to go to camp?" I searched my brain, trying to remember if he had mentioned camp. Maybe I hadn't been paying attention.

"It was kind of last minute. Uncle Martin came through. He's paying for camp."

I fidgeted with my fingers, trying desperately not to cry. "Can you meet me in the barn when I do my chores tonight?"

He hunched his shoulders. "I don't know, Quinn. Your dad was pretty clear I couldn't see you."

"He won't know." I was practically begging. I couldn't let Maiken leave without explaining why I'd been drinking, or hit Sloane, or made a mess of my summer.

"I better not. I just stopped by to check on Celia. I have to go. My mom is waiting. I have a few last-minute things to get before I head out in the morning."

I shoved down the tears. "Wait. You're only here to see Celia? You mean you weren't going to tell me you were leaving tomorrow?" One tear slipped out, then another as my stomach churned.

He glanced around, his blue eyes filling with frustration. "Quinn, I was going to call you."

"Why don't I believe you?"

"I don't know. But if you didn't get drunk, I would've told you about camp."

"So now it's my fault?" I asked in a harsh tone even though I was ready to beg him to stay.

He gave me a sad, or maybe pitying, grin. "We'll talk soon. Give my best to Celia." He spun on his heel.

I rushed up and latched on to his arm. "Wait."

He narrowed his big blue eyes. "I have to go, Quinn." There was no emotion in his tone at all.

My heart disintegrated. "Are you breaking up with me?"

"I'm going to basketball camp, nothing more. But I don't like you drinking. It's not something I'm going to deal with." Then he strutted out.

I was left with a crushed soul and a bleeding heart. I wasn't sure our relationship would ever be the same.

Chapter 8

Maiken

I wiped the sweat from my brow with my jersey. Between running suicides and the summer sun beating down on the outdoor court, all twelve of us were dying. The last two weeks had been brutal on my body and on my mind. I couldn't shake the thought that Quinn and I had had our first fight.

I was mad at her for getting drunk. I was mad at myself for walking away. I should've stayed and told her about camp, but the way she'd acted had given me the impression that no matter what I said, she would only see that I was leaving her. She knew how important basketball was to me.

"Take a break and hydrate," Coach Green yelled. "Maxwell, can I see you for a minute?" He waved his fat hand at me.

Noah, my roomie at camp, and a hell of a shooting guard, widened his gray eyes as though he knew something I didn't.

I couldn't imagine that I was in trouble. I'd followed the rules and busted my butt in workouts, training, and mock games. I even obeyed curfew when Noah didn't. He'd tried to get me to sneak out with him, but I wasn't about to mess up my training.

I jogged up to Coach.

He patted the spot on the bench next to him. "Sit."

I'd learned my first week at camp that Coach Green was the sports director at Greenridge Academy, the same school Mom was looking into for Jasper and Marcus, the same school she was trying to convince me to consider.

At first, I'd thought Mom and Coach Dean were in cahoots when it came to picking this camp, which was only a town over from Greenridge Academy. As it turned out, though, Coach Dean was the one who'd recommended the camp.

"If you want to get back into fighting form, then spend a month at basketball camp," Coach Dean had said. "I know Coach Green well, and he will whip you into shape."

Coach Dean hadn't lied either. Coach Green was like a military commander. We were up at dawn, running and working out before we had breakfast. Then we had two hours of classes on the game of basketball and plays. After that, it was off to practice on the court.

I eased down on the wood bench as I watched the guys fan out to the coolers.

Coach chugged from a water bottle then set it down. "I want to discuss something with you." He sounded like he was about to break bad news to me.

My pulse ticked up a notch. Maybe I was a terrible ball player. Maybe I didn't stand a chance of playing for a Division I school.

I started moving my foot, causing my knee to bounce up and down. "Just give it to me straight." I didn't like when anyone beat around the bush.

"I would like for you to consider attending Greenridge Academy for your senior year as starting shooting guard. I've talked to Coach Dean about this."

I whipped my sweaty head at him, probably causing my brain to suffer from whiplash. "You have? He's okay with me leaving?" A pang of hurt spread throughout my chest. Coach Dean had said he had big plans for me and the team. He and I had talked about the upcoming season, practices, the captain's role, the new guys on the team, and even about state championships.

Coach Green lifted up his ball cap, swiped a hand over his short salt-and-pepper hair, and then returned the cap to his head. "I know this sounds like it's terrible news, but I struggled with my decision. Coach Dean and I are good friends. The last thing I want to do is steal his players. But he assures me he's fine with me making the offer. He wants to give you the best opportunities. Look, Maiken, I know you had a terrible season last year. Coach Dean tells me you've been working your tail off. And I see it here. I'm highly impressed with your dedication and work ethic. You have great potential to play for the NBA one day."

His compliment dulled the pang in my chest and validated all the long workouts, the endless hours of shooting ball, and the days of pushing myself to the brink of pain even when I knew I should've taken breaks.

Sighing, I glanced up at the clear blue sky, saying a prayer to Dad, who I hoped was watching over me. I longed to have him there, talking to me, giving me advice, helping me make the hard decisions, deal with girls, everything. Sadly, he wasn't.

I swallowed down the emotions clogging my throat. I wasn't there to get teary-eyed. I was a young man who knew what he wanted, at least in the next phase of his life after high school.

"I know this is sudden," Coach Green said. "Just think about it. Talk to Coach Dean. I'll show you around the school this weekend as well. We're playing a scrimmage with the Greenridge team. Then afterward, you can make your decision. Fair enough?"

That was more than fair. I found the timing suspect, though, since Mom was considering the school. "Coach, have you been talking to my mom?"

Lines dented his high forehead. "Not at all. Should I?"

I chuckled. "Nah. She's been looking into Greenridge for us this year."

He raised an eyebrow. "Really?"

"She feels the school would be good for her five teenagers."

"I see. Greenridge is a great school and well known for preparing students for college. We have a great ROTC program for those interested in the military, and we have smaller classes than public schools. Every student who attends Greenridge is given a job on campus, from tutoring others, to working in the cafeteria, to leading and managing new students."

I wasn't interested in ROTC, although if basketball didn't pan out, then I'd always thought I would follow in Dad's footsteps.

"Has your mom visited the school yet?"

"She's supposed to in the next week or so. I guess my cousin Kross is supposed to accompany her and the family."

He rose, fingering his whistle. "Kross is a good egg. He did well while at Greenridge."

I wouldn't exactly know, although he was a big-time boxer.

"Let's invite her up this weekend," Coach said. "I'll show her around. For now, get something to drink and think about our conversation."

"Yes, sir. Coach, what about the other guys? I'm sure they would like the same opportunity. Noah in particular."

Noah and I hadn't talked much about his background except that he'd moved twice in the last three years. His mom accepted temporary assignments with the company she worked for, which kept them traveling around like gypsies.

Coach smoothed a hand over his somewhat big belly. Word from some of the boys who'd attended his camp last year was that he liked beer. "None of them are as good as you, son. And I need a shooting guard." He blew his whistle.

The guys jogged over.

Noah pulled me aside as I headed over to get some Gatorade. "What's up, dude?"

"Coach wants me to attend Greenridge this fall."

He slapped me on the back. "For real? That's great."

"What would you do?" I asked. "You've heard of the school."

He ran his fingers through his black hair. "I would take it, man. Lots of guys from there have gone on to play in the big leagues."

I grabbed a drink. "Why don't you enroll?"

"Noah. Maiken," Coach called. "Hurry up."

I discarded my cup in a box Coach had set out for trash.

"My mom is taking a new assignment this fall, so we're moving from Syracuse," Noah said. "She hasn't found out where, though."

"Wouldn't it be easier if you went to a school like Greenridge since your mom travels a ton?"

He shrugged. "Maybe, but it's not that simple."

I'd tried to get Noah to open up, but as soon as we started talking about family, he always shut down. So our conversations tended to revolve around sports and general topics of nothing. I had mentioned I had a girlfriend, but I didn't go into details. He didn't want to talk about family, and I didn't want to talk about Quinn.

We joined the group.

"All right," Coach said. "You boys did well today, and it's time to put some of the things you've learned in the last couple of weeks to use. We'll be playing the Greenridge basketball team this weekend at the school. That means we have three more days to go through the techniques you've learned in practice. I'm proud of each one of you. Now get back to the hotel and shower. We'll meet in the lobby at five for dinner."

The guys scattered, chatting as they collected their gear.

Noah tapped me on the arm. "Let's head to the pool to cool off."

Some of the others around us agreed, perked up, and asked if they could join us.

"The more, the merrier," Noah said.

The hotel we were staying at had a nice pool and Jacuzzi. My muscles could definitely benefit from the Jacuzzi.

I grabbed my bag from the grassy area behind the basketball goal. "I'm in. I just need to make a call first." I plucked my phone out of my bag and turned it on.

Noah jogged up to Brady, another guy who hung out with us in the evenings.

I tapped on Mom's number as we headed to the hotel, which was less than a mile away.

"Maiken," Mom answered, excitement lacing her tone. "How's camp going?"

I'd spoken to her a couple of nights ago, but Mom was always eager to hear my voice. "Good. You're not going to believe this. Coach Green wants me to play for Greenridge this year. Did you talk to him?"

She laughed. "I don't know Coach Green, honey. I sense you're considering it, though."

I walked along the perimeter of the park, following a good distance behind the guys. "It's pretty up here. Lots of trees and rolling hills."

"But?" she asked.

"I kind of had my heart set on playing my last year with Kensington and for Coach Dean."

"I see," she said. I could picture her staring out the window, her mind working overtime to find her next words. "I've made a decision. Jasper, Marcus, Emma, and Ethan will be attending Greenridge next year. At first, I was only considering Marcus and Jasper, but Emma and Ethan have expressed interest in the school. Financially, it might be tough at first, but with my job at the law firm now, I should be able to swing tuition."

"So Ethan wants to go to Greenridge?" I hadn't spoken to my brother except a text here and there about Celia. I'd been happy to hear that she was doing better and was out of the hospital.

"He does. You know he's leaning toward the military, and Greenridge has a great ROTC program."

I shouldn't have been surprised. Ethan had been talking about the military since he was a little boy.

"Maiken," Mom said. "I don't want you to attend Greenridge because you think you have to babysit your siblings. Make the choice for you and not anyone else, not even Quinn. You have one year to get scouts to notice you."

A horn blew, making me flinch and orient my vision. I found myself about to cross the street without looking. I gestured to the driver with my hand that I was sorry as I backtracked onto the sidewalk.

"Everything okay?" Mom asked.

"I'm good. I'll think about it, Mom. By the way, Coach Green invited you up to watch our scrimmage game at the academy this weekend."

"Oh? I wasn't planning on touring the school for another week, but

I can pile the family in the car and head up. I'll let Kross know since he was planning on coming with us."

"Cool. I've got to run."

"Maiken, I love you," Mom said. "And I'm very proud of you. I know if your dad were here, he would be too." Her voice cracked on the last sentence.

"I know he would." A tear stung my eye. "I miss him."

"We all do. But remember what I told you—he's with you every step of the way."

My chest hurt whenever we talked about Dad. "Love you too, Mom. I need to go. See you this weekend." I hung up before I started bawling like a baby.

I glanced around and tried to shake off my emotions.

The hotel peeked out from behind the shops on Main Street. A few people went in and came out of the coffee shop next to me.

I inhaled and waited for the crosswalk sign to light up.

My mind worked overtime, rifling through the pros and cons of attending Greenridge or staying at Kensington. The only pro I could come up with for Greenridge was their basketball program.

Despite the tension between Quinn and me, I didn't want to leave her. I didn't want to break her heart. Yet I'd made a decision to pour every ounce of energy I had into basketball. So now was the time to buck up.

Chapter 9

Quinn

I gawked at the beautiful rolling green lawn of Greenridge Academy. In some way, the campus reminded me of the farm, but without the scent of manure and hay.

I walked up to the edge of the parking lot, where the grass met the asphalt. A handful of cars were pulling in. Maiken's mom had wrangled Jasper, Marcus, Ethan, and Emma into a small huddle behind me, talking family stuff that I didn't need to hear.

I was desperate to see Maiken. He didn't know I was coming. I'd asked his family to keep it to themselves, although I didn't know if any of the boys or Emma would blab to their brother. I suspected Marcus would since he and I weren't on good terms.

Nevertheless, I wanted to surprise Maiken, and if I were being honest, I was afraid if he knew I was coming, he would tell me to stay home. We hadn't spoken since he'd left. However, we had swapped a few texts. Nothing of great substance filled our messages back and forth except that he was learning a lot. I owed him an enormous apology. I'd acted like a huge brat that day he'd shown up at the hospital.

A car door slammed a moment before Emma sidled up to me. She flipped the tail of her ponytail over her shoulder and let it drape down her chest. Her light-brown hair was off-the-charts long, and she'd grown at least two inches since school let out. Before long, she would be as tall as Maiken. She was already approaching Ethan's height, which was about two or three inches shorter than Maiken, who was six foot two. Marcus and Jasper weren't far behind either.

"This place is pretty lit," she cooed as the sun glinted in her big brown eyes and sparkles of her makeup glistened.

I hated to agree with her. I didn't want to see Maiken leave Kensington or Ashford or me, but as excited as Emma was about attending a rich private school, I was afraid Maiken would jump on board with her and the rest of his siblings. I'd learned on the way up that he was considering the move, something he hadn't mentioned to me, not even in a text, which was adding to my fear, nerves, and brooding.

No one in the car had revealed which way Maiken was leaning. Their mom didn't even know. Or maybe his family was afraid to tell me, although I hadn't asked. I was too frightened of the answer.

As I took in the beautiful campus, which reminded me of a place fit for a king and his court, I had a feeling Maiken would follow his brothers and sister.

I was ready to bawl and beg him not to leave. Actually, I'd cried for two weeks straight after he left me standing in the hospital with my mouth hanging open and a hole in my heart. Even though we had kept in contact with one another, I felt as though we were growing apart.

"I don't like you drinking. It's not something I'm going to deal with." His words had been on repeat in my head.

"Give him space," Momma had said when I'd cried in her arms the other night.

Momma and Daddy were still beyond livid at what I'd done, and I was still grounded until further notice.

The only good news was that Celia was doing well and was out of the hospital. The doctor had mentioned that she might not remember much, but she did. She'd told me every detail of that night, including jumping on Sloane's back. Since then, though, she was taking it easy. We hadn't done much of anything. I couldn't even have Celia over to hang so she could help take away my misery over Maiken.

Emma slipped her hand in mine. "My brother loves you, you know?"

I squeezed her hand. "Thank you for that." Her words were like a

balm to my somewhat broken heart. But I would rather hear the sentiment from Maiken. I'd thought many times since Maiken left for camp
that he didn't love me anymore. "He hated seeing me tipsy."

She giggled. "You mean flat-out drunk." She laughed again. "You
shocked all of us. Good Girl Quinn did something no one ever
expected."

"I'm not sure I'll do that again either. My dad would keep me
locked up forever." I wasn't kidding. I inhaled the scent of fresh-cut
grass. "You're excited about going here, huh?" It was time to change
the subject. I would rather not talk about the hell I was going
through or think about how Celia could've died from her head
injury.

Emma glanced around. Her happy expression and the gleam in her
eyes said it all. "They have a great volleyball program. But it's more
than that. My family hasn't settled since our dad died. I hate leaving
my mom and my little brother and sisters, but I think us older kids
could use a place like this."

I captured my trembling bottom lip in between my teeth. "Maiken
included?" I knew her answer. I just had to hear her say it.

"Yeah. Sorry, Quinn. I believe he needs a school like this more than
any of us. He's bottled up all his feelings over Dad's death, and he's
put everyone but himself first. If he wants to play ball and focus, this is
the place for him to get his shit together."

She sounded older than her seventeen years. Or maybe I was still a
little girl who wanted to be in love and not have anything change in my
life. I knew the Maxwells had moved constantly when their dad had
been in the military. But for a hometown girl like me, who didn't travel
or move around, I would not want to be away from my family or my
boyfriend.

But you will when you go off to college. Even that was going to be
difficult for me.

I didn't want to cry, but I had a feeling I would be bawling before
the day was out. "Is Maiken as excited?" I wasn't sure if she'd talked
to her brother about the school.

Emma let go of my hand and gave me a sidelong look. "Even if he decides to attend with us, that doesn't mean he's breaking up with you."

I shuddered at the thought, although I wasn't exactly certain we were boyfriend and girlfriend. "I won't see him, though. We're supposed to spend our senior year together at the same school." *And fall in love harder and deeper, and have sex for the first time, and kiss, and make out, and not come up for air until we're heading off to college.*

The boys and Christine ambled over.

Jasper, who I hardly knew or spoke to, was now a high schooler. At fifteen, he was tall for his age and resembled Maiken. They both had sandy-blond hair and similar features—strong jaw, nose, lips, and a soft gaze—except Jasper's eyes were brown rather than blue. "Maybe you should transfer here with us." Even his voice was similar to Maiken's.

Suddenly, I wanted to throw my arms around him. He had a gentle way about him, unlike Marcus. "My parents wouldn't allow that." Besides, with Carter and Liam in college, I was the only one there to help my parents on the farm.

Christine dumped her keys in her purse then smoothed a hand down her crisp cotton slacks. "Let's head in. Coach Green said he would meet us in the main building."

Marcus started for the entrance of the castle-looking building. "This place looks like something out of Harry Potter." His voice kicked up a notch, and his swagger screamed excitement.

Color me surprised. Marcus was usually brooding or had a pout on his handsome face.

The Maxwell clan was happy. Even Ethan had a pep in his step as he and Jasper talked about dorms and living on campus.

The world around me seemed light, airy, and gleeful, while I was the one sulking. Not to mention, I felt like a school of piranhas was nipping and biting inside me as my nerves crept up over thoughts of seeing Maiken.

Would he be as happy as his siblings? Would he be happy to see me?

We wound our way down a tree-lined path to the gray stone building with pointed peaks and towers jutting up into the sky. The closer we got to the massive portico, the more my heart pounded in my ears. With the mountains and dense landscape surrounding the property, I felt like I was entering Hogwarts.

The double wooden doors opened as we approached, and an average-looking man with salt-and-pepper hair greeted us. "You must be Christine." The older gentleman extended his hand.

Christine exchanged a handshake with the man. "Coach Green?"

"Please, call me Robert." He gave her a warm smile, or maybe he was smitten with her. After all, she was a beautiful lady. Her dirty-blond hair was swept up in a chignon, and a light dusting of makeup accentuated her small nose, big brown eyes, and full lips. "Let's go inside." He waved his hand to the open door.

The Maxwell kids went in first.

I lingered behind, suddenly feeling like I was intruding.

The coach eyed me. "Christine, do you have five teenagers or six?"

Christine smiled warmly at me. "This is Quinn Thompson, Maiken's girlfriend."

Wrinkles creased Coach's brow. "Maiken didn't mention he had a girlfriend."

I held my stomach, feeling like I'd just gotten punched in the gut. I swallowed a big knot and plastered on a fake smile when all I wanted to do was puke, cry, and run for the trees.

"She's part of the family," Christine said.

Yep, I was going to cry.

Coach Green grinned, showing his pearly whites. "Nice to meet you, Quinn. I'm sure Maiken will be glad to see you."

Pfft. I doubted that, but Coach's words gave me a small kick in the pants to walk into the building. As soon as I did, the scent of frankincense hit me. I felt like I'd just entered church.

The Maxwell kids were milling around, inspecting the row of portraits hanging on the wall outside an office.

"We'll take a tour of the property," Coach said as he and Christine came in behind me. "First, I'll take you folks to see Maiken. The game doesn't start for a couple of hours. So we have plenty of time." Coach Green waved us on. "This way."

With Coach and the Maxwell kids leading the way, we navigated long hallways and passed offices.

Christine walked alongside me. "Quinn, are you okay?"

I shrugged. "Yeah," I lied. The closer we got to seeing Maiken, the more my stomach spun into a web of nerves.

She patted my arm. "Whatever Maiken decides, we need to support him. I know this is hard for you. It's hard for me. But he needs basketball. I know he can play for Kensington. Here, though, he might have a better chance of getting into a good college."

"Maybe. But Liam got into NC State, and that's one of the best colleges in the country. I don't see the big draw here except maybe the property."

She pursed her lips, losing her smile.

"I'm sorry. I know you want what's best for Maiken."

"Quinn." Her voice was a smidge harder than usual. "If you love my son, then you'll want what's best for him no matter what."

I did love Maiken, beyond what words could describe. I also wanted him to live his dream. Yet I felt like I wouldn't be part of his dream.

"Honey," Christine said in a softer tone. "Maiken loves you. And if the love you both have for each other is strong, then nothing, not even distance, will break that bond. I know. I was a military wife. And the time away from my husband was rough, but our relationship grew stronger and stronger. Not only that, each time he came home, it was like a honeymoon all over again."

"It's just hard. I don't want him to leave Ashford."

She smiled weakly. "I don't either."

So many emotions rifled through me. In one breath, I was overly excited to see him. In another, I wanted to run back to the car. I inhaled, hoping to calm my nerves.

Before long, we were walking into the gymnasium. My mouth gaped at the state-of-the-art gym. White hardwood floors traveled the length of the court, appearing like a sheet of ice. Two TV screens hung from the high ceiling at midcourt. Bleachers surrounded all four sides like those in a college or NBA stadium, and on one side of the gym, the afternoon sun spilled in through the bank of windows that lined the top of the wall.

A group of boys congregated around the basketball hoop at the far end.

I searched for Maiken but didn't see him. His siblings climbed the bleachers and found seats, which wasn't hard. The gymnasium only had a handful of spectators scattered around.

I joined the Maxwell siblings and sat next to Jasper.

He nudged me. "There's your boy."

My gaze darted out to the court. Maiken wiped his brow with his jersey, showing his six-pack abs, as he emerged from a tunnel in between the stands in the corner.

I quietly sighed and swooned. When his gaze darted in our direction, I waved.

His jaw dropped, and his blue eyes gleamed. I wasn't sure if he was happy to see me or not, but I was going with yes because he had an easy grin.

All the worry, sleepless nights, inability to eat, and nonstop crying vanished as my heart sputtered. The boy I'd met in my farm store that November of our sophomore year, the one who made butterflies take flight, the boy who had eyes as blue and deep as the ocean off the coast of Florida still had my heart to touch, to hold, and hopefully to keep.

He jogged over. His sweaty hair was stuck to his neck and forehead, and his muscled biceps bunched as he lifted his shirt again to wipe off the moisture from his face. "Hey." He regarded his siblings. "You guys are really going to like the school."

My heart bounced down the stands and onto the floor.

Christine left Coach Green's side and headed straight for Maiken. "You look like you're having a great time." She hugged her son.

"I am, Mom. It's been a great experience."

Then she leaned in and whispered something in his ear before she joined us and took a seat next to Emma.

Maiken finally set his blue gaze on me. "Want to go for a walk?"

I swallowed the elephant in my throat and willed my pulse to quiet down. Otherwise, I would be throwing myself at him and begging him not to leave Kensington. Before I could wallow in my sorrow, I stood up. "Sure."

We walked side by side, not touching. There were no hugs, only silence, as he guided me through a side door that led to a courtyard.

Again, I was wowed. Umbrella-topped tables were sprinkled around the cozy closed-in area. A massive grill that Daddy would be envious of was the focal point as the sun glinted off the stainless-steel top. And flowering trees provided shade in just the right spots. The place rivaled an outdoor dining facility at a high-end restaurant.

"It's good to see you," Maiken said, keeping his distance as he sized me up. "You look as pretty as ever."

I certainly didn't look like death as I had that morning in the hospital. I smelled better for one, and I was dressed in a pair of capris, cute flats, and a flowery blouse.

I threw myself at him. "I'm sorry about my party. I'm sorry I was such a bitch to you at the hospital. Don't leave. Please stay at Kensington." I was officially a wild woman and a basket case. Tears poured out like I had no control of my emotions.

His hands dove into my long hair. "Hey." He pressed his body to mine, finally wrapping his arms around me.

I sighed so heavily, I swore I was ready to scream or burst into a song.

He hugged me tightly. "It's okay. I'm sorry too. I shouldn't have walked out without talking to you. I was shocked that you were drunk."

I nuzzled into the crook of his neck, absorbing his heady scent that was a mixture of soap and sweat. "It won't happen again." I'd said those words a thousand times to my parents and to myself.

Stepping back, he grasped my hands and locked eyes with me. "I know, Quinn." He swallowed. "I can't do drinking."

I nodded. "I'm never touching the stuff again."

He gave me a sexy grin. "But I hope you'll touch other things." He waggled his eyebrows.

My cheeks burned like an inferno as I replayed that quiet interlude we'd had on the side of the barn. "Me too."

He laughed, sounding relieved and free. "You realize we kind of had our first fight."

I gnawed on my bottom lip. "It felt more like a breakup than a fight."

He gave me a smile that made me feel gooey and warm. "I do love you."

I threw myself at him again. "You don't know how much I needed to hear that. I love you to the stars and back."

His body vibrated with laughter as we held each other for a long moment before he released me. "I haven't made a decision yet on whether to attend here or not. I actually wanted to talk to you about it."

I pinched my eyebrows. "Really? I just told you not to leave Kensington."

"True. But that's your emotions talking. Believe me, Quinn, I don't want to be miles apart from you, but I might have a better opportunity here to get seen by scouts."

My hands shook. "Then you should join your brothers and sister." I didn't want to whine or be a big baby, even though I would miss not seeing him in the halls at Kensington or stealing a few minutes in between classes in our little hideaway supply closet.

He tugged me across the ivy-entwined, lattice-covered courtyard until we were on a curved stone bench.

"This school looks expensive," I said through a sniffle.

He rubbed the back of his neck. "I guess. So you're not grounded anymore?"

"I am. Your mom convinced my mom to let me come with her." I'd been surprised Christine was able to get Momma to say yes. Like Daddy, she hadn't gotten past her disappointment, and for a very good reason.

My party had been the gossip at Sunday Mass, and my parents hated when we were the talk of the town. Daddy was a proud man, and he wanted everyone to know the Thompson family didn't cause trouble. He also felt that we could lose business if folks had a bad taste in their mouth with us.

Regardless, Momma hadn't given me a good reason as to why she'd agreed to let me go. My theory was that Christine had told her Maiken would be leaving in the fall and it would be good for me to see him one last time.

"What will you decide?" I asked.

Maiken hopped up and shoved both hands through his hair. "It's a tough decision, Quinn. I don't want to leave my mom either." He squatted down and placed his hands on my legs. "It's not like we're breaking up." Pain etched his handsome features.

It sure feels like we are. "I know. But I won't see you every day."

He chuckled. "I doubt you will even if I stay at Kensington. We don't take the same curriculum. After school, I'd been planning on joining a community basketball league to keep my skills sharp."

I leaned in and kissed him. I didn't want to talk. I wanted to kiss and feel how much he loved me.

His tongue dove inside my mouth, taking and tasting.

I whimpered as I tangoed with him.

Nibbling on my lip, he broke the kiss. "I love you. Nothing will change that."

I wasn't so sure. I had the sinking feeling the separation would drive a wedge between us, but I couldn't deny Maiken his chance. I couldn't stand in the way of his dream. I wasn't that type of girl. Yet that didn't mean I wouldn't bawl my eyes out.

Senior year was about to suck the big one.

Chapter 10

Maiken

Four weeks of camp flew by, and I had a decision to make. I'd wavered back and forth on attending Greenridge. Seeing the sadness in Quinn's eyes when she'd visited me at the academy had torn my heart to pieces. But I really liked the school. I liked Coach Green. I'd gotten to meet the basketball team, and the guys seemed nice. I also didn't get the sense that they didn't want a new guy taking over their territory or that there were any big egos at play.

Oddly, I felt at home at Greenridge Academy. I felt like I belonged there. For so long, especially since Dad died, I hadn't felt whole. I'd been feeling lost, trying to find myself, and worrying about taking care of my family.

Coach Dean was talking to Mr. Thompson as I pulled into the lot at the farm store. I'd called Coach, and he'd told me he had a few minutes to chat before his weekly poker game with Mr. Thompson.

Mr. Thompson was wearing his normal scowl as he listened to whatever Coach Dean was saying. I cut the engine and glanced out at the farm, hoping to catch a glimpse of Quinn. As far as I knew, she was still grounded. But my search came up empty. No one was milling around the horse barn or even outside the house.

I climbed out just as Mr. Thompson went into the farm store.

"Let's take a walk," Coach said, swiping a hand over his shiny bald head.

The summer heat had been brutal with high humidity and a heat index that was off the charts.

"How was camp? Coach Green tells me you were great."

We ambled down along the perimeter of the farm and settled near the small building Mr. Thompson used to sell Christmas trees.

"Did he also tell you he wants me to play for him?"

"He did. And you should consider his offer, son."

I angled my head. "You don't want me playing for you?"

He looked past me briefly. "I do. Look, Coach Green has the best connections with scouts and colleges. He even has friends in high places. Plus, the school will be good for you. You'll do nothing but study, attend classes, and train."

I knew he was looking out for my best interests, yet I couldn't help but feel a pang of hurt in my gut. "I like the school."

Coach Dean tucked his hands into his pants pockets, studying me. "But? What are you afraid of?"

I squinted at the setting sun. "Leaving my mom. Quinn."

He gripped my shoulder. "As you should be. But think about yourself. What do you want, Maiken? I mean, look into your crystal ball. What do you see for yourself? Not for anyone else, but for you. Don't worry about me, your mom, Quinn, or anyone. I want you to dig deep and find what's going to make you happy."

My eyes burned as tears filled them. What I wanted I could never have. I wanted my dad there, having the same conversation with me that Coach and I were having. If he were there, he would be asking me the same thing.

"I want to play for a Division I school. I want my dad to be proud of me. I want my mom to be as well. I want a family in the future. I want to play in the NBA. Most of all, I need Quinn in my life."

He smiled like a proud dad. "Then pour your heart and soul into the game. Through your hard work and dedication, everything else will follow—family, girlfriend, NBA."

"You sound so sure."

He chuckled as he started back toward the farm store. "You've been through a lot, son. It's time you focus on you."

"You think Greenridge will help me do that?" My gut said yes. But I wasn't so sure about my heart.

"The academy will remove all the noise surrounding you and allow you to zero in on your talent. Think of it as basketball camp for an entire year."

The four weeks at camp was comparable to military boot camp, or I suspected as much given what Dad had explained about his time in boot camp. Regardless, a regimen-like camp for a whole year would get me in tip-top shape to play ball. Maybe then I would have several options when it came to a full ride to a Division I school.

We stopped outside the farm store.

"I better get inside," Coach said.

Mr. Thompson poked his head out. "We're about to start." Then he looked at me as if he knew my question. "Quinn is down in the barn or maybe feeding the pigs."

"Sir," I said to Mr. Thompson. "I didn't drink that night." I'd been wanting to get that off my chest.

Mr. Thompson cracked a smile. "I know, son."

It was weird to see him smile. I wasn't complaining, though. "Thank you."

"Let me know what you decide," Coach Dean said before he moseyed inside.

My head spun as I headed down to the barn. *Do I go? Or not?*

Go. You know you want to.

But what if Quinn decides she doesn't want to wait for me? Or what if some boy snags her attention this year?

I was near the barn when her sweet and flowery voice slithered into my ears. Basketball and decisions could wait.

"Beast, get back in your pen," Quinn ordered the pig.

I laughed as I watched her wrangle the fat animal into the pig pen across the way.

She spun on her heel. "You're home." Then she ran like she was in the fifty-yard dash and launched herself at me.

I caught her, steadying us so we wouldn't fall.

She peppered kisses on my cheeks, forehead, nose, then mouth. She lingered for a long minute on my lips. "I've missed you."

Well now, maybe I should go away more often.

She slid down my body, the friction causing my jeans to tighten. "When did you get back? How come you didn't call me?"

I seated my hand on her lower back, making darn sure she didn't move an inch, not because of my boner, but because I missed the heck out of her. I missed the feel of her against me. I missed her bright smile, her big amber eyes, and her butterscotch hair. But most of all, I missed kissing her.

I crashed my mouth to hers and took, tasted, and devoured. She melted into me like butter on warm toast. When her tongue clashed with mine, I forgot where I was, and frankly, I didn't care that I was standing in the middle of her farm for anyone to see.

Her dad could pry me off her, or try, but I wasn't letting her go, not in this minute, hour, or lifetime.

My breathing was all over the place. My hands were in her hair, on her butt, her body, and her arms before cupping her face. "I've missed you terribly."

She whimpered before pulling me over to the side of the pig pen where no one could see, not even her mom if she was watching from the house.

She shoved me against the building, giggling. "Let's resume where we left off on the night of my party."

Holy shit!

"Um... Your brothers?" Liam hadn't left for college yet, and I doubted Carter had either.

"They're at the gun club."

My muscles loosened.

She fumbled with my belt.

"You're not drunk?" I knew she wasn't, but she'd never been this forward sober.

She rolled her eyes, unzipped my jeans, and was about to slip her hands inside when I stopped her.

Confusion filled her eyes. "What's wrong?"

I circled my fingers around her wrists before bringing them up to my chest. "We need to talk." I couldn't let her take advantage of me then tell her I was leaving.

Beast snorted as he came around the corner of the building.

Quinn giggled. "This pig is the bane of my existence."

Beast pushed his snout into my leg as though he were giving me a warning. *Don't you dare hurt my girl.*

A laugh broke out in my head at the absurdity of what I was thinking about a darn pig.

Quinn tapped Beast on the butt. "Come on. You need to eat."

Beast followed her as she guided him into the pen with the other pigs.

I was right behind them with a smile from ear to ear. It was amazing to see how animals responded to her. I still wasn't ready to ride a horse, but I didn't have a problem with pigs.

Once Beast was in, Quinn locked the gate. "Where were we?"

"Talk," I said.

She pouted, and that plump bottom lip jutted out. "You're going to Greenridge, aren't you?"

"Honestly, up until I walked down here, I kept changing my mind. But after talking to Coach Dean..." I tugged her to me. "Please understand."

Tears pooled in her pretty eyes. "It hurts."

I caught a tear as it escaped. "I know. I need to do this. You can come up to visit me, and I'll come home when I can. Plus, I'll be home for the holidays. And you can throw yourself at me and do whatever you want."

Tears cascaded down her cheeks as she giggled. "Whatever I want, huh?"

I bobbed my head, my groin responding.

She slumped her shoulders. "Senior year won't be the same. We can't sneak into our little hideaway and steal a kiss or cop a feel."

My phone buzzed in my pocket. I suspected it was Mom. She wanted me to babysit my younger siblings while she got some work done. She was working on an important case.

But when I took out my phone, Noah's name lit up my screen.

I raised my finger to Quinn and mouthed, "One minute." Then I slid the icon on the phone to answer. "Hey, man. Can I call you back in a bit? I'm with my girl."

"Sure, but make sure you do. I have something I need to talk to you about." He sounded serious.

"Give me an hour," I said before hanging up.

"Who was that?"

"A friend from camp." I'd wanted to introduce her to Noah when she visited me at Greenridge, but Noah had a family emergency he'd needed to deal with.

Quinn rubbed the toe of her shoe in the dirt. "When do you leave?"

"Friday."

"What? Like in three days? Why so soon?"

"Greenridge starts a week earlier than Kensington." I held out my hand. "Come here."

She shook her head. "I can't."

I felt as if she'd just stuck a knife in my chest. "Why not?"

She pouted. "Because I won't let go."

I wrapped my arms around her anyway. "We'll talk on the phone. We'll text all the time, and we can even FaceTime. You know, we might be doing just that anyway when we go to college."

She tensed against me. "I thought we had one more year before we went our separate ways."

"Maybe we'll both get accepted to the same college," I said, unsure of myself.

She gave me one of her shy and sexy smiles. Man, she looked like a farm goddess. Strands of her hair were wild around her face, her nose was red, her cheeks were flushed, and her cleavage was on display in her ratty V-neck tank top. "Maybe. You know, we should have sex before you go."

I choked.

She eased away. "What? You don't want to?"

My mouth instantly went bone dry. "Fuck yeah."

"So what's with the panicked look?"

"I get the feeling you want to have sex because I'm leaving. I don't want to rush into it. Sex is a big step for both of us, Quinn."

She twisted her lips. "I know. I still have to talk to my mom about the pill anyway."

That was another reason she hadn't been ready to take the plunge.

I stepped closer to her. "So we're good?"

She stuck out her tongue at me, her shyness bleeding through the redness in her cheeks. "Yes."

I heaved a sigh, even though it was going to be excruciatingly difficult to say goodbye to her.

Chapter 11

Quinn

My sweaty skin trapped pieces of my hair to my neck and forehead. The weather for late August was disgustingly humid. We didn't have air conditioning, so the nights had been unbearable. Momma and I had found ourselves on the front porch, lying on one of two swings, which both had comfy cushions and pillows, hoping to catch a cool breeze on most nights, but none came. Daddy and my brothers didn't seem to mind and slept through the heat.

I was ready for ten feet of snow and subzero temperatures. The heat coupled with Maiken leaving for Greenridge had me irritated and antsy beyond belief.

He'd been gone for four long days, and I couldn't stop crying. I couldn't sleep, and I couldn't even eat. Celia had tried to cheer me up, but nothing was working. It hadn't even helped when Daddy lifted my punishment.

Things around me were changing, and I didn't like it one bit. I'd lost my boyfriend to a private school. Liam had left for NC State the day before, and Carter was returning to Boston in a matter of minutes. Then I would be the only one at home.

Momma had cried last night and again that morning when Liam hugged her before getting into the car with Daddy. I even cried as we waved when they drove away.

"I'm not sure I'll survive when you leave next year," Momma had said. "I'm losing all my babies. The house feels empty already."

I rocked on the porch swing, staring out at Carter's beat-up truck, wondering what Maiken was doing at that moment. His classes had started the day before, and he hardly had time for much with school-work and practice.

The screen door creaked open. "Quinn." Momma still sounded sad. "Why don't you help me with dinner?"

Blinking, I tore my gaze away from the chipped red paint of Carter's truck and regarded Momma. "I'm not hungry."

She wiped her hands on her apron, giving me a pitiful look. "Have you called Maiken?"

"We texted." No amount of texts or phone calls would erase the pain I felt or the loneliness setting in. "Momma, what if I never see him again? What if Maiken doesn't want to go out with me anymore? What if he finds another girlfriend there?"

She smoothed a hand over her dark-brown hair as she sat on the edge of the swing next to me. "Oh, honey. If the love between you two is strong, then no one can break that bond, not even another girl."

"It hurts too much. Sometimes I can't breathe."

She rubbed my leg. "He's your first love, and those are the most painful, but they're also very special. Why don't you call Celia and invite her to spend the night? It will help to take your mind off Maiken."

Sniffling, I pulled away. "I might just take Apple out." My horse always seemed to put me in better spirits.

Momma curled strands of my hair behind my ear. "I think that's a good idea."

Carter came out with a suitcase in one hand and his phone in the other. "I'm leaving now. See you then."

Momma rose. "Why so soon?" Her voice was even sadder than before.

Carter set his suitcase down on the wooden planks of the porch. "Brianna and I want to get a head start before traffic picks up for the Cape."

My mom kissed Carter on the cheek then gave him a hug. "You be careful. I want you to text me that you made it safely. Understood?"

"Yes, ma'am."

She breezed back into the house.

"Still brooding?" Carter asked. He was decked out in shorts, flip-flops, and a Boston University T-shirt, looking tanned, relaxed, and eager to see his girl.

I stuck him with my middle finger as a bucketload of jealousy soured my stomach. He was going to see his girlfriend and have a great time at the Cape while I was stuck at home with chores and loneliness.

Jeez, Quinn. Pity much?

"My advice, for what it's worth—play the field, sis. Date. Have fun."

I rolled my eyes. "You don't understand love, do you? And having fun? You saw how that went down at my party." Plus, I couldn't date. Maiken and I hadn't broken up, although it felt like we had.

Carter stalked closer before resting his butt on the railing. "I'm not saying get shit-faced. You can go to a party without getting drunk. Besides, aren't you still set on making valedictorian?"

I knitted my eyebrows. "Of course. What does that have to do with Maiken or having fun?"

"Between doing my job and Liam's on the farm and studying, you won't have time to see any boys, let alone Maiken if he were here."

"You're just a bag of fun. Not." Although he had a point. Until Daddy hired someone to help out, it was little ole me and Daddy. Momma would help, but she had her hands full with the farm store.

"If you need anything, Quinn, call me. You hear me? I'll be there for you." Sincerity threaded through every word.

I snorted. "You've never been there for me before unless you were scaring away boys. So what changed? Are you looking for a reason to not go back to school?" He'd told me he was thinking of quitting.

"Not at all. In fact, I've decided to give it one more year before I make my decision on whether or not to continue."

"My advice is to get your degree."

He hiked a shoulder. "I gotta run. Brianna is waiting." He closed the distance between us and kissed me on the forehead. "Be good."

I laughed. "Maybe I won't this year."

"It's your funeral." He chuckled as he headed to his truck.

I envied my brother. I wanted to pack a bag and drive up to Greenridge.

Carter beeped the horn and waved as he drove off.

My phone rang beside me, and Celia's name lit up the screen.

"Want to spend the night?" I rushed out. Loneliness was setting in like a bad virus, seeping into every vein, making me feel ill and sad.

"Look out at the top of your driveway," Celia said.

I squealed as she drove slowly down and parked in the spot Carter had just vacated. I hung up, vaulted off the swing, and ran down the porch steps.

Celia had barely gotten out of her car before I threw myself at her. She smelled of the beach and coconuts.

"Were you tanning?" I asked.

Her arms went around me. "I was earlier."

I held on to her like she was my lifeline. In a lot of ways, she was. I only had Celia now.

"Quinn, you're hurting me." She giggled. "I'm not leaving you."

My body vibrated. I was on the brink of bawling for, like, the millionth time since Maiken had left.

Celia leaned against her car, looking as pretty as ever with tanned skin, cute red-painted toes, flowers on top of her flip-flops, and her hair up in a bun. Big hoop earrings complemented the beach vibe she was exuding. "It's time for you to stop pining over Maiken. Tessa's having a pool party tonight. It's her end-of-summer bash. Let's convince your mom to let you go."

I scrunched my nose. "Are you kidding me? My mom will tie me up before she lets me go to another party."

Her button nose wrinkled. "You're not grounded anymore. Right?"

"My dad lifted my punishment last week. Still, I'm afraid to ask."

She pushed off her car. "Let's ask your mom together. You'll thank me later when we're jumping in Tessa's pool. This heat is unbearable."

A refreshing swim might do the trick. I chewed a nail as I followed my bestie into the house. "Mom?"

"In the kitchen." Mom's voice competed with the sound of the TV in the family room.

Celia walked in before me. "Hi, Mrs. Thompson."

Mom stirred a pot of spaghetti sauce. "Celia, honey. How are you?" She set the wooden spoon down on the counter.

"I'm good. Mrs. Thompson, do you mind if Quinn accompanies me to Tessa's pool party?"

Mom rounded her gaze to me so fast I thought her head would spin off.

"I won't drink," I quickly added. "I promise."

She lifted her chin, studying me like she was trying to get inside my brain.

I pressed my palms together in prayer. "Please, Momma. It will take my mind off Maiken. If I come home drunk, you can ground me until I graduate."

She mashed her lips into a thin line. "Your father will have a stroke if he finds out."

"He won't," I said.

Momma wagged her finger at me. "Quinn, I want you home by midnight. No later. Do you hear me?" Her tone permitted no argument. In fact, she sounded like she would lock me in my bedroom if I so much as had a drop of liquor on me or was one minute late.

I jumped up and down, and for the first time since my party, that suffocating feeling disappeared. "Thank you, Momma."

She gave me a stern look that could melt ice. "Don't make me regret my decision, Quinn Thompson."

An hour later, Celia and I were walking into Tessa's mansion, dressed in our bathing suits beneath sundresses with our bags in hand.

"Born to Be Yours" by Kygo and Imagine Dragons belted out of the speakers. One room after the next was filled with kids.

"This party is rockin'," Celia shouted over her shoulder.

Tessa greeted us at the outdoor kitchen area and shoved two red cups at us. "Drink."

I arched a brow at my former enemy. "Does that have any liquor in it?"

She rolled her dark eyes. "Are you for real? Of course it does."

I shook my head. "Not drinking."

She stuck her hand on her bare hip. Tessa was sporting the tiniest bikini, and she looked fab in the red fabric, which barely covered her boobs. "It's a rite of passage. Just sip it. Don't pour it down your throat like you did at your party." She talked to me as though Celia and I were in Liquor 101 class.

Dustin Lane waltzed up, his swim trunks resting low on his hips. He wasn't wearing a shirt, showing off his six-pack abs. He ran his long fingers through his thick, wet black hair. "Quinn, how's Maiken?"

I growled low under my breath. I didn't want to talk about Maiken. "Good." I swiped the cup from Tessa and drank a mouthful, then choked. "This is straight alcohol."

Tessa laughed so hard, she cried.

Dustin kissed her neck. "Babe, that wasn't nice."

I snarled at Tessa. "Do you want a repeat of your Christmas party?"

Dustin cocked his head at his girl. "What happened?"

"The water isn't cold," Tessa said, still sporting an evil smile. "So do your worst."

Celia snagged a red cup from Tessa and dumped it in the small sink. Then she took mine and did the same. "We're not drinking. Come on, Quinn. Let's mingle." After Celia's two-day hospital stay with a severe concussion, I didn't think she would ever drink again. I couldn't blame her either.

Dustin wrapped his arms around Tessa from behind and began nibbling on her ear. "You don't have to be such a witch."

"Oh, come on. It's fun to see Quinn get all feisty."

I stuck my middle finger at her. "Do you really want to revert back to enemies? Because if you do, bring it on."

Tessa rolled her eyes before she twirled in Dustin's arms, and then the two began sucking face.

I joined Celia, who was lingering around the packed pool of kids drinking and talking. Outside the pool, more kids lounged on chairs or blankets while a group of boys putted on the makeshift green on the other side of the pool.

Celia tapped me on the arm as we dodged a group of girls huddled together as though they had a huge secret. "Who's that?"

I oriented my vision. "Who?"

Celia leaned in. "He's sitting on the edge of the pool. Black hair, sun-kissed skin, flowered swim trunks. And he's staring in our direction."

My gaze bounced around until I found the guy she was talking about. "He looks like Dustin." I couldn't see his eyes all that well, though, with the late-afternoon sun beaming directly at him.

"Yum," Celia cooed.

Dustin was a hottie. "I wonder if he's related to him?"

A hefty boy threw a girl into the pool, and the impact caused a tidal wave. Water went everywhere, including on Celia and me.

Normally, I would get mad, but the water felt nice on my sticky, heated skin.

Celia tore off her sundress, exposing the tiny bikini covering her curves and big boobs. "Let's go in."

I was usually the shy one who didn't like to show off too much skin, but I was becoming braver with age. Maiken had had a lot to do with increasing my self-esteem. Besides, we were there to have fun.

When I removed my dress, Dustin's lookalike was suddenly in our faces.

Celia straightened her spine. "Hi." Her tone rose in pitch.

I internally rolled my eyes at my BFF as she went into flirtation mode.

The group of girls who had been whispering shuffled closer to us.

"Hi, ladies. I'm Noah." He pinned his gray eyes on me.

Celia extended her hand. "I'm Celia, and this is my best friend, Quinn."

While still looking at me, he shook Celia's hand and said, "You must be Quinn Thompson."

Celia angled her head. "How do you know Quinn?"

I sucked in a breath. "Have we met before?" It was a stupid question, but maybe we had.

Noah flicked beads of water, or maybe sweat, from his broad, tanned chest. "I've heard a lot about you."

My eyebrows disappeared into my hairline. "From who?"

"Yeah. From who?" Celia parroted.

Noah stabbed a thumb at Dustin and Tessa. "Dustin. He and I are cousins."

I would've bet on brothers. Still, what could Dustin possibly tell Noah?

OMG! My party!

Heat pinched my cheeks as embarrassment set in. *He must think I'm easy since I drank too much. Or maybe he just likes me. Or maybe Dustin has a crush on me.* A laugh broke out in my head. No way Dustin had a crush on me.

"Well, she has a boyfriend," Celia said firmly.

Noah stared at me, totally ignoring Celia. "Really?"

I narrowed my eyes at him. "Yes. I have a boyfriend."

One side of Noah's lips curled. "That's not what I hear."

We weren't in school yet, and the word had already spread about Maiken and me.

I crossed my arms. "My boyfriend may not be here, but he's still my boyfriend."

He flicked his head ever so slightly as though he didn't believe a word I'd said. "Well, Quinn Thompson, see you around." He strutted off in the direction of his cousin. His long, muscular legs ate up the pool deck until he was seated at a stool behind the bar where Dustin was flipping burgers and Tessa was pouring a drink.

"OMG! What was that all about?" Celia asked.

"No clue." I was flattered, but that was the gist of it.

Celia's eyes darted to Noah. "If you ask me, he's crushing on you for sure. Although I wouldn't mind crawling up his tall body."

My phone rang, and I fumbled to get it out of my bag.

Celia looked at my phone. "Go someplace quiet."

With my phone pressed to my ear, I headed away from the party and toward a cluster of trees in the backyard. "M-maiken?" I stuttered, something I hadn't done in ages.

"There's my girl." His Southern drawl sent delicious shivers down my arms. "Sorry I haven't called before now. I've been practicing and working out and studying. Two days of classes and practice, and I'm already beat to a pulp. How's the love of my life?"

I was a thousand times better now that I was listening to his raspy tone.

Chapter 12

Quinn

The bell chirped, announcing the end of my second class on the first day of my senior year.

Ugh! Depressing was how I would describe the day so far. I was looking for Maiken any chance I had. I was so used to seeing him strut down the hall or come up from behind and kiss me on the neck or ear.

Kids spilled out into the halls, and the buzz of voices and laughter ricocheted off the metal lockers. Girls huddled close together. Boys gathered in groups, eyeing the girls close by. Others walked to their next class, looking like zombies out of *The Walking Dead*.

I felt like a zombie. With Carter and Liam at college, I had the pleasure of doing their chores too. I had to get up an hour earlier to help Daddy with the animals. Four a.m. was not a time to be crawling out of bed when all I wanted to do was snuggle under my blankets and sleep until graduation.

Sighing, I hiked my bag over my shoulder, dodging students as I made my way to AP Biology. Most of my classes that year were advanced placement. I had to keep my head down and study hard if I wanted to maintain my high grade-point average and stay on track for valedictorian. I had ticked the boxes so far for the esteemed honor at the end of my junior year. If I kept up my perfect grade-point average, I shouldn't have any problems.

I passed Jessica Bento, who was holding a ladder while her cheerleader mate Elise Davis tacked a banner to the wall above a bank of lockers.

Smoothing a hand down her cheer uniform, Jessica's big blue eyes went wide before she waved me over. "Hey, Quinn."

I tucked my hair behind my ear, sliding in and out of traffic. "So we're playing Forest Grove in our first football game, huh?" At least that was what the banner read. They were one of our big basketball rivals, but their football team sucked according to Liam.

She shrugged. "Have you heard from Maiken?"

That was an odd question coming from her until I remembered she had the hots for Ethan. At least I assumed she did since I'd seen them together at my party.

"I have." Maiken and I had spoken a few times since he'd called during Tessa's party.

She stuck out her pink bottom lip. "Ethan won't text me back. I've tried to call him too, but he won't answer." She puffed out her cheeks. "I don't know what to do. I'm going nuts. I thought he liked me, but I'm getting the feeling he doesn't want anything to do with me."

I sympathized with her. It had been maddening when I'd repeatedly texted and called Maiken the night of my party with no response from him. "Maiken says they're busier than ever with sports and school." One week without Maiken seemed like a lifetime of hell.

A boy ran by me, bumping me in the shoulder and almost body checking me into a locker.

"What the hell?" I shouted.

The tall black-haired boy with wide shoulders stopped, turned, and hustled back to me.

I did a double take. "Noah? You go to this school? Since when?" After we'd briefly met at Tessa's, I hadn't paid much attention to him. Celia and I had hung out, people watching mostly. In fact, Noah hadn't stayed at the party that long. He'd left before Celia and I had.

Elise had already climbed down while Jessica and I had been chatting. She flipped her long brown hair over her shoulder and grinned at Noah like she wanted to eat him. I could understand the swooning she was doing. Noah was definitely droolworthy, but he was not my type, even though Celia kept saying he liked me.

Whether he did or not, my heart was taken by a sandy-blond-haired boy who was my everything.

A mischievous grin lit up Noah's handsome features. "Since today. My mom took a job in town."

"Are you a senior like Dustin?" I asked.

Elise stared at Noah, her hungry brown gaze piercing into him and pleading for him to glance her way.

Jessica was fiddling with her phone, more than likely trying to get ahold of Ethan.

Noah shook his head, his unruly black hair falling into his eyes. "Junior. But I'm late. I need to get to the admin office. Do you know where that is?"

"I'll take you," Elise piped in quickly, flashing a radiant smile.

He finally regarded her with a lack of interest. "Thanks. So, Quinn, do you want to hit that burger place in town after school?"

Elise's cheeks slowly darkened as she shot daggers at me, daring me to say yes. If I did, she looked ready to cut off my head. Luckily, she had nothing to worry about.

"I told you—I have a boyfriend," I said to Noah.

He kept his expression neutral. "I understand. I'm just looking for a friend."

Presume much, Quinn? What a ditz I am.

Elise hooked her arm in Noah's. "I'll go with."

Noah didn't acknowledge her. Instead, he gave me a pleading look, much like Elise had given him.

I could use another friend. "I can't anyway. I've got a ton of chores on the farm."

"Farm? Do you have horses? I love horses," he said, not giving up.

Jessica tapped Elise. "Let's go. We need to finish what we started, or else Tessa will be chewing our butts off."

"Noah." Elise gushed his name, batting her long, thick, mascara-laden lashes up at him. "The admin office is this way." She stuck out a blue-painted nail, pointing down the hall behind her.

Celia bounced up out of nowhere. Her red lips were set in a tight line, and her eyes were narrowed behind her brown-rimmed glasses. I guessed she didn't want to wear her contacts. "There you are."

Noah gave me one last cheeky grin and reluctantly left with Elise tethered to his arm and Jessica leading them.

"Was that Noah?" Celia asked.

"He goes to our school now. What's with the snarly look?"

"I guess we have several hunky new boys this year," she said, watching Noah fade around a corner.

I snapped my fingers. "Focus. You're confusing me. You seemed upset, and now you're swooning."

"You're not going to believe this. Sloane Price is in school, and she has a brother too. A hot, yummy brother."

Here we go. Now that Celia wasn't dating Liam anymore, she was on the market and on the prowl. I remembered her exact words: *"I don't want to be tied down. I want to date who I want. So does Liam. I also want to explore more of me."*

Since Maiken had left for the academy, I couldn't shake Celia's words, and only because I was praying Maiken wouldn't meet a girl at Greenridge and feel the same way as Celia and my brother.

"Wait. I thought Sloane moved."

"Not the point," Celia fired back. "Hunky brother. Tall, big biceps, to-die-for smile, shaggy blond hair that curls on the edges around his ears, and eyes the color of dark emeralds."

"So Sloane isn't moving?" She'd probably convinced her mom to stay in Ashford so she could get revenge for me punching her. "Let's not forget what she did to you."

"I did jump on her back," Celia said, sounding frustrated with me. "Speaking of your party, did you know Sloane's brother was at your party?"

Considering I hadn't exactly been coherent, I wouldn't have noticed. I opened my mouth to ask her again if Sloane was moving or not when a scream tore through the halls, piercing my eardrums.

Some of the kids lingering in the halls cringed and froze while others searched for the girl who had lungs worthy of a horror movie. Just as the girl's scream died, a loud boom rattled the lockers.

Before Celia and I could move, someone shouted, "It's a gunshot."

Suddenly, mayhem broke out. Kids ran for cover and into classrooms. Some even stopped to look, trying to see if anyone truly had a gun.

Celia grabbed my hand. "Let's go."

I let her tug me, even though I was certain the boom wasn't from a gun. "It's a firecracker." I raised my voice over the collective squeals that grew louder as we melded into the herd of students.

Another boom echoed, followed by a series of crackles.

Tessa barreled toward us, her arms flailing like a flag in the wind. "Get out of the way. There are pigs chasing us."

I stopped in my tracks, causing Celia to almost fall into me. "Pigs? What?" I caught Tessa as she was about to run by. "Where?"

More screams followed.

"Oh my God! Get that disgusting thing off me," a girl squealed.

"It's one of your pigs," Tessa barked, showing perfect white teeth. "Why would you bring pigs to school?" Her tone was so high it could shatter glass.

I laughed so hard I had tears in my eyes. I didn't know why I was laughing when she was accusing me. "Now why would I do that?" I was beyond curious who would actually do that and why.

Celia nudged me as she pointed at a girl pinned against a locker by none other than my sweet pig, Beast.

I wiped tears from my eyes, my fit of giggles dying a quick death. My first thought was that Daddy was going to have someone's head on a platter, and I sure hoped it wasn't mine. The way bad luck was glued to my butt, I was sure I would be the one to blame.

I strutted toward my pig as the hall cleared out in an instant.

Beast snorted, sniffing the blonde's leg. So many questions pummeled me at once. It almost made my brain hurt.

"Beast," I said sweetly. "Now how did you get here?"

"Who cares?" the blonde cried. "Just get the disgusting animal away from me. I hate pigs."

I crouched down to Beast as I addressed the girl. "They are one of the sweetest and smartest animals."

Beast pushed his nose into my hand as the blonde bolted down the hall.

"More pigs are coming!" Tessa shouted at the top of her lungs. "Quinn, you're evil. They're going to kill someone."

I gritted my teeth as Godfrey, my spotted black pig, came up to Beast, followed by Momma's favorite, our white pig, Lola, the runt of the three. Momma occasionally let her into the kitchen when she was cooking a roast. Lola loved carrots.

"Oh, please," Celia said. "Pigs don't kill."

I didn't have to look to know that Celia had rolled her eyes at Tessa.

"Why do they have numbers painted on them?" I asked.

The only people in the hall besides me were Celia and Tessa, who was hanging on to Celia for dear life.

"How did they get here?" Celia asked.

That was the million-dollar question.

Footsteps clamored down the hall before Dustin appeared and marched up to us. His eyes were wide, but something about his grin was off. "What in the world? Must be a senior prank." Dustin bent down and petted Lola. "She's cute."

"What do you mean, senior prank?" I asked.

"Why else would they be here?" he asked as Tessa slinked up, seemingly brave all of a sudden.

It figured she wouldn't show how scared she was in front of her boyfriend.

Celia commandeered Godfrey, who had a mind of his own, trotting down the hall in the direction of the cafeteria. "Come on, little guy. We need to get you out of here."

High heels clicked on the floor behind me. "What the hell?" Principal Sanders's voice blared.

I blanched as I shuddered. With my luck, I would get suspended because the pigs belonged to me.

The principal loomed over me as I petted Beast. "Whose pigs are these, and why are they in my school?"

"They belong to Quinn," Tessa rushed out. "She probably did this."

I snarled at the girl I wanted to strangle. "You probably did this," I fired back, even though Tessa wouldn't go near a farm animal to save her life.

Tessa half smiled. "I wouldn't dirty my hands with these disgusting creatures."

Dustin cocked his head at his girl as if to say, "Really?"

Whatever.

Principal Sanders arched a dark eyebrow. "Quinn, explain."

I rose to my full height. "The pigs are mine, but I have no idea how they got here."

"Why do they have numbers painted on them? I see one, two, and four. Does that mean we're missing a pig?" She pinned her gaze on Celia, Tessa, Dustin, and then me. "Is this your idea of a senior prank?"

I shrugged. I had no clue what the numbers meant.

Beast pushed his snout into Principal Sanders's leg, getting snot on her slacks. She didn't flinch in the least.

"I doubt there's a third one," Dustin said with Lola at his feet.

The principal glowered at him. "How do you know this?"

"The numbers on them are designed to confuse you so that you think there's a fourth pig. I only know this because I saw this prank on some TV show."

Principal Sanders wasn't buying his theory, as indicated by the crinkles around her gray eyes. "Let's get them out of the school before I have the health board here, shutting us down. Quinn, call your father."

"He's not home. My parents went up to New Hampshire for the day." They were looking at a new horse, and Momma wanted to shop for some new items for the farm store. She'd even closed up for the day to go with Daddy.

"I have my truck," Dustin said. "If I had a ramp, we could get them in."

The principal pulled out her phone from her suit pocket. "I'll check with the janitor."

I peeked into a classroom. "This one is empty right now. Let's get them in here."

Celia wrangled Godfrey. Dustin had Lola, and I got Beast. Tessa bit her nail as she watched.

Once inside, I sighed. "My dad is going to have a cow, literally."

Celia brushed her palms on her shorts. "My money is on Sloane. She's probably getting back at you for punching her."

That made sense, and she had lived on a farm. Therefore, she knew how to wrangle animals. But I didn't understand how stealing my pigs and dumping them in a hallway at school would be any type of revenge. The whole charade of a senior prank was just that—a senior prank. Unless she thought I would get expelled or suspended.

At the moment, it didn't matter who was responsible. I needed to call Daddy, and he wasn't going to be happy.

Chapter 13

Quinn

Dustin and I managed to get the pigs back to the farm and return to school just in time for our last two classes. I'd probed him all the way to the farm, but he hadn't seen anyone dropping pigs off at school or lighting off fireworks. I tried to remember if I'd seen anyone in the hall, but I hadn't.

On the way back to school, I called Momma and Daddy to fill them in. Daddy was grunting and growling as Momma informed me they would be cutting their trip short. I told her not to since the pigs were okay, but I knew Daddy wouldn't listen. The farm and the animals were our livelihood, and Daddy didn't take kindly to anyone messing with his property.

I didn't either. The pigs could've gotten hurt or killed. I adored my animals. Momma had always said not to name them. "Once you do, honey, you're attached, and with pigs, you can't let that happen, since we use them for food or sell them."

She was right, although Godfrey, Beast, and Lola had been with us for a couple of years. Daddy knew I was attached. I think he spared them just for me.

Now as I sat in class, I tapped my foot on the floor at my desk, waiting impatiently for the bell to ring. The first day of school was a complete success. *Not!* I'd been wracking my brain on who would have pulled such a prank.

Celia was certain Sloane had a hand in it. My theory was that anyone could've done it. Dustin agreed with me. And Tessa? Well, her money was on me. I'd wanted to stuff a sock in her mouth. The girl wouldn't shut up about how disgusting the pigs were. She'd almost tagged along with Dustin and me earlier, but she'd had some cheerleading thing at lunch. *Thank God.*

The intercom crackled in English class before a sweet lady's voice came through. "Quinn Thompson, please report to the admin office."

I doubted Principal Sanders was going to be that sweet. Sometimes I wondered how she put up with a school full of teenagers.

Kids peered over their shoulders at me, snickering. They probably thought I was in trouble. I didn't see how I could be. But stranger things had happened. If anything, Daddy would give me the stink eye and then grumble about how teens had no respect for their elders or other people's property. Plus, I could hear him say, "If we didn't have that darn party, we might not have kids stealing pigs for their own enjoyment."

Guilt burned like acid in my throat. I should've taken the hint that parties were a bad omen for me. After all, every one I'd attended so far had ended in some type of disaster. At Tessa's holiday bash two years ago, I'd ended up in the pool during the dead of winter. Homecoming last year had resulted in Maiken getting hit by a car.

I scurried out before the throng of kids packed the halls. I was anxious to find out who I needed to yell at. Oh, I was going to rain down on someone's parade.

As mad as I was, the others in school seemed to be enjoying the video that had gone viral of Beast pushing out his snout and holding the blond girl hostage.

I'd heard one boy in passing say, "This year is going to be wild."

Not in my book. I just prayed tomorrow would be better than today. Then again, without Maiken at school or living in town, my life sucked.

I wound my way down three halls before opening the glass door into the admin office.

Ms. Hobbs, the principal's new assistant, lifted her head from her computer. "Have a seat, Ms. Thompson. Principal Sanders is in with someone at the moment." Then she set her glasses on her long nose and went back to her computer screen.

I slid my backpack off my shoulder and sat down in one of four wooden chairs. "She's not in with my parents by any chance?"

Ms. Hobbs peeked around her computer, her blue gaze landing on me. "No. Students."

The clock on the wall read three thirty. Momma and Daddy should be home by now. I took my phone out of the back pocket of my shorts and sent Momma a text.

Me: *Are you and Daddy back yet?*

Momma: *We are. The pigs are fine. All the animals are good.*

Me: *Great. I'm waiting to talk to the principal to find out who did this.*

Momma: *I hope she tells you. Your father is furious. He's talking about pressing charges.*

I wasn't surprised. I took in a deep breath just the same. I was all for making sure whoever was responsible paid for his actions, yet I couldn't help but feel a pang of pity for that person.

The door opened to Principal Sanders's office.

Me: *Gotta go. Celia is giving me a ride home.*

Oh crap. I forgot to remind Celia to wait for me. I quickly sent her a text, and just as I hit send, Sloane Price's voice filtered out before she did.

I lifted my head as my phone fell to the floor. I had yet to see her in school. I'd thought maybe Celia had her rumor all wrong.

Sloane's white-blond hair had grown out and down to her shoulders, and her silver-studded nose ring shined beneath the overhead light. She was glancing over her shoulder. "Yes, ma'am." Her voice was light, sweet, and anything but snippy and condescending, which was her usual MO. "Trevor, come on. We're late." Then she pivoted on her heel and locked eyes with me.

If she had any bruises from where I'd punched her over a month ago, they were long gone.

I snagged my phone before I rose, leaving my bag on the floor. "Are you responsible for the senior prank with my pigs?"

One side of her red lips ticked up as a boy two heads taller than Sloane came up behind her. His emerald eyes and shaggy hair told me he was the boy Celia had described to me that morning. He looked at me as though he'd found a new puppy.

My intuition was telling me to stay as far away from him as possible. He had one of those grins that was downright evil. I swallowed thickly, wishing upon a star that Maiken was at my side. I wasn't a coward, but the boy gave me the creeps. Sure, he was off-the-charts gorgeous, but that didn't mean squat.

He pushed past his sister, practically throwing her to the side, and strutted the short distance over to me. "You must be Quinn Thompson. I barely remember seeing you at your party. Shame. I would have danced the night away with you."

I giggled for nothing more than to do something with my nervous energy. I knew if I opened my mouth, I would stutter, and no way was I about to do that. That boy was a bully, or as Granny would say, a piece of work.

I craned my neck up, my heart ready to push its way out of my chest. I wasn't attracted to him. In fact, I was a bit frightened. There was something about him I couldn't put my finger on. Maybe it was his size. He was as wide as he was tall and had huge biceps, just like Celia had described.

"Do you speak?" he asked.

Sloane joined her brother and touched his arm. "Leave her alone, Trevor." She sounded like she was afraid for me.

I could feel my eyebrows coming together as I regarded her, but she wouldn't look at me.

"Ms. Thompson," Principal Sanders called. "In my office."

Saved by the principal.

I picked up my bag and started to slide around Trevor, but he blocked me.

I narrowed my eyes at him. I might have been about to pee my pants, but he wasn't going to see me sweat. "Move." I couldn't believe that one word came out steady.

A slow and wolfish grin emerged. "She does talk." He moved a stray hair of mine that was stuck to my cheek behind my ear, slowly dragging his finger as though he were getting off on the act alone. "I'll see you around, wild one."

One of my eyebrows went up, like way up. I felt as though I needed to sprint home and take a shower. "You have me mistaken for someone else."

He leaned down and whispered, "Not in the least." Then he gave me a wide berth.

Shivering, I hurried into the principal's office like a mouse being chased by a cat.

I could hear Sloane speaking in a low voice. "Don't mess with her."

I let out a nervous laugh as I sat down in a chair in front of the principal's desk. Normally, I would wait for permission and practice manners, but to hell with that. My legs were trembling.

Calm down. He's only trying to scare you. I just didn't know why.

I blew out a breath, puffing out my cheeks. It was official. This might be the worst school year of my life.

Principal Sanders finished scribbling notes and set her pen down. "The reason I called you in this afternoon is because I have an opportunity for you."

"Wait. Have you found out who's responsible for the senior prank?"

She clasped her hands on her desk. "We haven't, and unfortunately, the one camera we have outside the cafeteria door isn't working."

"Someone had to have seen the pigs on campus before they came into the school."

"We're checking with students and faculty."

No student would tattle on another student. It would be social suicide.

"We'll get to the bottom of it." She sounded confident.

I didn't. "My dad wants to know." I stabbed my thumb behind me. "So Sloane and Trevor didn't have anything to do with it?"

"Sloane's stepbrother just enrolled." Principal Sanders always made a point of having a sit-down with new students.

"I guess she isn't moving, then," I mumbled to myself, clenching my fists. Maiken wasn't going to be happy about that. But at least Marcus was at the academy now, and Sloane was in Ashford, which meant Sloane might not cause trouble without Marcus around. Her stepbrother, on the other hand, might.

I stood. "I'll let my dad know."

She held up a hand. "We're not finished."

Oh yeah, opportunity.

I resumed my seat.

"I understand you're on track to make valedictorian. Normally, the guidance counselor would be having this conversation with you. But Mrs. Flowers is out for the next month on personal leave. Until I find a temporary replacement, I'm handling some of her workload. I would like you to tutor this year. It will help your college applications."

I did need an extracurricular activity other than being on the math team. I wasn't sure if I had time to tutor, but with Maiken gone, my afternoons were free other than my own studying and chores on the farm.

"Do you have someone in mind?"

"Trevor Thames."

No way on this planet. I cocked my head. "The boy who just left your office?"

She nodded. "He's behind in some subjects since he missed the last two months of school in his sophomore year. If he can catch up on his math and English, then he can finish as a junior this year."

"Does he know you want me to tutor him?"

"Not yet. I wanted to be sure you would agree to it first."

I hated to disappoint Principal Sanders. She'd always been nice to me, and I also wanted my college applications to look good.

"Can I check with my parents?" I didn't have to, but considering I was the only one at home to do chores and help Daddy, it was a good idea to run it by them.

"Sure. Let's revisit this topic tomorrow, then."

"Again, if you hear anything on the prank, can you at least call my dad?"

She pressed her red lips together with a hint of a smile. "In this town, nothing stays hidden for long."

I couldn't agree more. Daddy had a way of finding out things before me sometimes. Besides, with the way kids gossiped around school, it was just a matter of time before the truth came out.

But the prank was the least of my worries. I had to find an excuse not to tutor a boy who scared the pants off me.

Chapter 14

Maiken

My legs were like Jell-O as I walked up the stairs to my dorm room, feeling spent from a hardcore practice. Every morning and afternoon, Coach Green had us training and working out—suicides, jumping jacks, push-ups, running laps around the track, basketball lessons, plays, and tapes of other teams. I was living and breathing basketball and school. I barely had time to sleep. I wasn't complaining, though. I was in the best shape of my life. My back wasn't giving me problems, and I didn't have time to wallow in how I was missing Quinn, although I did think about her every chance I had.

I missed catching a glimpse of her pretty face and sweet smile in between classes. I missed the quiet moments we'd had in one of the supply closets at Kensington last year.

When I dragged my butt into our dorm room, I saw Ethan with his back plastered to the wall and his knees raised as he lounged on his bed.

"No football practice?" I tossed my gym bag on the floor and flopped down on my bed.

Our room wasn't anything to write home about. It was just a simple setup with two beds, two dressers, two desks, and a window that overlooked the sports complex. A communal bathroom was located at the end of the hall, as well as a common room where we could watch TV or hang out.

Ethan lobbed his phone into my lap. "You have to see the video Jessica sent to me."

I sat up. "Of?" I hit play, and my eyes widened. "What the? Pigs in school?" I immediately recognized Beast. "Are those from Quinn's farm?"

Ethan dove into a fit of laughter. "I wish I'd been there. It's some senior prank."

"When did this happen?"

Ethan reached for his phone. "This morning. Didn't Quinn text you?"

I returned his phone and dug mine out of my gym bag, curious why Quinn hadn't called or sent me a text to let me know what had happened. Then I saw that I did have a text from her. "It looks like she did a few minutes ago."

Quinn: *I had a day from hell. How was yours?*

"What did she say?" Ethan probed, eager to hear more about the pigs.

"Not much. Let me call her."

"Before you do, I need to tell you something." His excitement died a quick death.

My pulse took a nosedive at his grim tone. Jasper, Marcus, and Emma were at school with us. Either Marcus had gotten into trouble, which wouldn't surprise me, or something had happened at home with Mom that I didn't know about.

Ethan scooted to the edge of his bed. "Sloane didn't move. Rumor is that her and her brother are responsible for the pigs."

I didn't like Sloane, although I got the attraction Marcus had for her. She was pretty, but man, she was trouble.

"Say what?" My brain was still processing the pigs in school.

"We can't tell Marcus."

I stared at Quinn's text message and the heart emoji at the end of her sentence. My own heart beat a little faster. Man, I was dying to see her. I would give anything to have her at school with me. If she were in the dorms, I could sneak out of my room and into hers.

Absently, I flipped my phone in my hands, my mind conjuring up images of Quinn and the sweet taste of her soft lips. An entire school year without her would be painful. Hell, the last week without her had been. What was I thinking?

You're doing this for your future, man.

"Bro, are you in there? Did you hear me?"

I inhaled the wooden scent that seemed to be imbedded in the walls, halls, and everywhere in the school. Actually, the school smelled like the inside of a church. "Yeah. We can't tell Marcus. But news flash —Sloane probably did already."

"Have you seen Marcus today? Because I didn't see him at lunch. He wasn't sitting with Jasper like normal."

I ran a hand through my hair. "Did you ask Jasper?"

"I didn't get a chance. Coach called an emergency meeting of the football team that cut my lunch short. Honestly, I didn't think much about it. I figured Marcus was running late, and Jasper was sweet-talking a girl anyway."

I chuckled. Jasper was making the rounds with girls for sure. I'd seen him a couple of times talking to two different girls that week. "Let's not worry about Marcus. He seems happy here, and if he's talking to Sloane on the phone, then let him." I was done worrying about him. I had my own goals and dreams to achieve—basketball, winning games, getting seen by a scout, prepping for upcoming scrimmage games, and doing well in my classes.

Ethan pushed off the bed and stood to his full height. "I need to ask Jasper something about football. I'll talk to Marcus, although soccer usually runs late."

That sounded perfect. I wanted to hear Quinn's voice anyway.

When Ethan reached the door, I asked, "Why are you so worried about him all of a sudden?" That job had been mine for the last year. "As I said, he seems happy."

Marcus had told me just the other day that he felt like he could finally breathe for the first time since Dad's death. In some ways, I agreed with him. There was something about the academy that was refreshing. I couldn't pinpoint what. I loved how Coach Green had taken me under his wing and made me feel like I'd been playing for

Greenridge since my freshman year. He also reminded me of my dad. Whenever he was frustrated because I'd messed up a play, he would address me by my full name. My dad had done the same when I'd been in trouble.

Ethan twisted the doorknob. "Mom needs our help."

I stiffened. He sounded as though Mom were sick, and the only thing I could think about was her sister, who had died last year of breast cancer. Mom had told me not long after my aunt's death that breast cancer was inherent in her family.

"Did something happen?" *Please say no. You better say no.* If Mom was sick, I was packing my bags right then and hitching a ride to Ashford.

"I haven't told you this, but before we left to come up here, I heard her crying every night." He heaved a sigh. "It just breaks my heart to see her sad and frustrated. As the older brothers, we need to step up."

"Weren't you the one who told me many times last year to take a chill pill?" I prodded him with my eyes. "Yeah. You were."

"Dude, I'm one year wiser. Besides, I hate how Marcus treats Mom with no respect. If Dad were here, he wo—"

"He's not." My tone was hard and raw and downright steeped in fury. I hardly got angry with Ethan, but his big-brother attitude all of a sudden was twisting a knife in my chest, making me feel like I didn't care anymore, and I did. Then again, I should be thankful he was stepping up. Maybe it was time for someone else to kick Marcus's ass.

A muscle jumped in his jaw. "Exactly. It's up to you and me. So deal with it." He stormed out, closing the door behind him with a loud bang that shook the walls.

I flung myself back on my bed, staring at the poster of the basketball court I had tacked to the ceiling. The picture was a reminder of what I was striving for—the scholarship, the full ride to a Division I school, making my mom proud, and even my dad, who I was sure was watching down over the family. Most of all, I wanted to play ball for the NBA more than anything.

"Stay focused," Coach Dean had said before I left.

But I didn't know how I could when I took one step forward and two steps back, or at least that was how it seemed.

I lifted my phone and tapped on Quinn's name. I needed to hear her sweet voice.

"Maiken." She sounded upbeat, excited, and relieved.

I quietly sighed, my body warming in all the right places. "Hey, babe."

"I miss you terribly. You're not going to believe what I have to tell you."

"First, I love you."

She sucked in a sharp breath. "What happened? Is something wrong?"

"Family stuff. Nothing like pigs in school." I discarded my brooding tone. She didn't need to hear about Marcus. Hell, she had to be tired of dealing with him and hearing me complain about my brother.

She giggled. "You saw the video. Everyone has seen that video. I'm sure when I go to church on Sunday, the whole congregation will be talking about it. I can hear them now. 'Kids. Who thinks of these silly pranks?'"

I didn't care what the churchgoers thought. I cared about my girl. "Tell me you love me."

"To the stars and back. I miss you so, so much. I want to see you."

Butterflies swarmed in my stomach. I wished I could reach through the phone and touch her. "I have a scrimmage game next month. Can you come up? I'm sure you could spend the night in Emma's room."

"Oh my God! Really? I would love to." Silence stretched over the line for a beat. "But I don't know if my dad will let me. I'll talk to my mom."

My fingers were crossed that her dad would say yes. "At least for the game." If I knew Mr. Thompson, he wouldn't let Quinn spend the night, knowing she was with me.

"My dad might agree to a day trip, and I'll ask Celia."

"Cool. So who unleashed the pigs?"

"No clue. Daddy is furious."

I propped up my pillow. "Did Sloane do it?" I couldn't see Sloane bringing pigs into school. She was a lot of things, but not somebody I could see doing pranks.

"You know she's not moving. Her stepbrother is going to Kensington. He's creepy too."

"Creepy?" I didn't like the sound of that.

"One of those guys who thinks his shit doesn't stink. The kicker is the principal wants me to tutor him. I haven't decided yet. With my brothers at college, Daddy has no one to help him."

"I wish I was there."

"I know. I miss our quick trysts in the supply closet." Sadness tinged her voice.

My heart broke. "I do too."

She sniffled, which was another blow to my heart.

I closed my eyes, envisioning her next to me. "I love you. But we'll be together soon. Holidays are coming up, and hopefully we'll see each other next month."

"The month will feel like years."

The week or so I'd spent away from her already felt like eons.

"Quinn," her mom called. "Dinner is ready."

"I have to go." She sounded like the world was ending. "I love you. Call me tomorrow."

Just as the line went dead, Ethan burst into the room.

My heart plummeted at the wild look he was sporting. "What did Marcus do?"

Jasper barreled in behind Ethan, guilt swimming in his brown eyes. "Sorry."

"Marcus isn't on campus," Ethan said. "He's in Ashford."

Several swear words blared in my head. "Does Mom know? Don't answer that. If she knew, she would've called me, or one of us at least. How did he get there?" Mom had a car, but none of us did.

Jasper dropped onto Ethan's bed, flicking his unkempt blond hair from his eyes. "Marcus heard Sloane wasn't moving. He convinced a guy on the soccer team to give him a ride. They left after lunch since practice was cancelled."

"Why didn't you come tell us?" I asked Jasper.

"Really? What could you or Ethan do? Marcus is Marcus, bro. I can't stop him, and I'm not going to try."

Ethan began to pace. "I tried to call him, but he's not answering."

I swiped a hand over my head. "Curfew is four hours away. If he's not back by ten tonight, then it's his ass."

Regardless, it was weird to see Ethan in freak-out mode. He'd always been the cool, calm, and collected brother. I was happy to know he would step into my shoes as big bro when I graduated.

Chapter 15

Quinn

Voices hummed in the cafeteria as kids ate and chatted.

Colorful leaves fell from branches, scattering to the ground directly outside the window near the table where Celia and I were sitting. The October weather was cold and brisk, and any remnants of summer and warm temps were gone.

Celia stabbed her fork into her wilted lettuce. "Aren't you going to eat?"

The overcooked pasta on my plate wasn't tempting my taste buds. "I'm not hungry." Since Maiken had moved up to the Berkshires, my appetite hadn't been normal.

I was also tired. I'd been struggling to keep my eyes open during classes for the last several weeks. Concentrating and listening to the lectures each day was brutal. I was even failing miserably studying at night.

With Carter and Liam not around to pick up the slack, Daddy and I were exhausted. I'd been a bit worried about Daddy too. He still wasn't in a good mood and hadn't been since my party. It didn't help that we hadn't found the person responsible for taking the pigs on the first day of school, which was eating at Daddy. He was thinking of installing cameras around the farm.

Celia shoved spinach into her mouth. "You should post the job opening for the farm on the school bulletin board. I'll also mention it in the school's blog. Someone will bite."

"I doubt that." First, Daddy was picky, and second, kids didn't want to clean out stalls and feed animals or get their hands dirty.

Coach Dean had had the basketball team working on the farm at the crack of dawn last year. Maiken hadn't complained, but some of the boys had, in particular Chase Stevens.

"I'd rather not have anyone from school." Sloane Price had applied last year, and that had proven to be a disaster, or rather she'd quit before she even started. "We need someone who is older and isn't afraid of hard work, someone with muscles to do the heavy lifting."

Celia ate her salad like she was starving. "Trevor Thames has muscles. Maybe you should see if he's interested."

I gasped at my BFF. "Are you insane? He's Sloane Price's step-brother. He's creepy, and he doesn't strike me as someone who's into hard work."

She wiped her mouth with a napkin. "I've been watching the basketball team practice, and he works hard on the court."

Trevor didn't strike me as the basketball type. He looked more like a linebacker with his wide shoulders.

"I hear he's looking for a job."

I shook my head vigorously. "No way. I want nothing to do with him." I'd only seen him in the halls here and there. Since he was a junior, I didn't run into him that much. When I had seen him, he was sucking face with a tall brunette.

Celia reached for her drink. "You have to admit he is yummy."

I scrunched my nose. "No way in hell." I would never acknowledge that she was spot-on. His dark blond hair brought out his striking green eyes.

"You know Elise Davis is tutoring him," Celia said.

"You're just full of all kinds of information. If I didn't know better, I'd think you want to date him." I guessed Liam was a blip on her radar now that they'd broken up. Then again, that was the point. They both wanted to see other people. Well, as far as I knew, Liam wasn't seeing anyone, at least he hadn't mentioned he was when I talked to him last week.

"Pfft. I'm the school's sports reporter. I need to know my players."

Giggling, I rolled my eyes. "You mean you're checking out every guy you can now that you're single."

She pushed out a shoulder, smirking. "Sue me."

We both laughed harder.

Principal Sanders had been quite disappointed in me when I respectfully declined to tutor Trevor. I knew tutoring would look good on my college applications, but not at the expense of my own studies. At least that was the excuse I'd given her.

"What about Noah?" I asked Celia. "You seem to like him too." Like Trevor, I hadn't had any more interaction with Noah since the first day of school. Again, we didn't see juniors that much in between classes. Plus, he seemed to have taken the hint that I was spoken for.

"So does every girl in this school. Basketball practice is like a Jonas Brothers concert. Girls are gathering in droves to watch Noah and Trevor."

I'd heard Coach Dean talking to Daddy the other night about how Noah was a great addition to the team. He hadn't said anything about Trevor, though.

"Hey." I narrowed my eyes. "Did Sloane ever apologize to you?" Sloane might not like me, but she'd almost killed Celia.

"Let's not discuss her ever." My friend gulped down her soda. "It's bad enough that when I get headaches, she comes to mind."

"Is the frequency of the headaches subsiding?" I still blamed Sloane for my party turning into fight night.

"I'm not having as many anymore," Celia said. "Back to the job on the farm. Think about posting a flyer. You need to get help, girl. Your valedictorian status is on the line."

I straightened my spine. I'd passed all my tests so far, but my grades hadn't been as stellar as they normally were. "I will. For now, can we talk about something else?"

She pulled lipstick out of her purse. "Are we still on for Saturday?"

I wasn't letting anything ruin my chances of seeing Maiken. "For sure." I pushed my tray away from me. "I can't wait to lock lips with my boyfriend." A delightful shiver blanketed me. It had been way too long since I'd seen him. "I can't stay the night, though." Daddy had shut the door on that pretty quickly.

The bell rang, which was our cue. I had a study period next, and I had to brush up on calculus before the test that afternoon.

Rising, I picked up my tray, as did Celia. After weaving through the incoming crowd and dumping our trash, Celia and I walked out. She went one way, and I went the other, in the direction of the library. On the way, I tapped out a text to Maiken.

Me: *I can't wait to see you this weekend.*

I was lowering my phone when I rounded a corner and plowed into a brick wall, or rather a hard chest.

I jumped back, holding my nose, just as big hands grabbed my arms. "I'm sorry." The boy's baritone voice made me cringe. "Are you okay?"

My eyes watered, and I swore I would give Trevor Thames two black eyes if I ended up with two of my own. "Can you watch where you're going?"

A wicked grin lit up his face, and those green eyes beamed with mischief. "You're the one with your head down. The way I look at it, I saved you."

My laugh bounced off the metal lockers. "How so?"

He slid to one side and pointed to the trash can. "You would've run into that."

"Do I owe you my life?" My tone was snarky.

He dragged his fingers along his sharp jaw, appraising me like I was his next meal. *Ew!* "Sounds like a good trade."

I tried to step around him, but he blocked me. I clutched the straps of my backpack as though they were my lifelines. "Excuse me. I have somewhere to be."

"So do I," he said. "With you."

This guy was a piece of work. "Go find someone who's interested."

I'd managed not to talk to him since the first day of school. I guessed my streak of bad luck was back with a vengeance.

A deep laugh rumbled free from the pit of his stomach. "I was actually coming to find you."

"I'm not interested." I didn't think he wanted my help with his schoolwork since he had Elise. She was a good tutor, or at least that was the rumor.

He feigned a pout and slapped a hand over his chest. "You really know how to hurt a guy."

I pursed my lips, my nostrils flaring like a bull ready to run at the matador. "Get out of my way."

Trevor stuck out his bottom lip. "You're not being polite."

"Pulease. Can you be any more fake?"

The hall had minimal traffic. Kids always lingered in the cafeteria until the final bell rang.

"Did you find out who brought your pigs to school?" he asked. His expression was a blank slate.

Somehow I got the feeling he knew. "Was it you? Rumor is your sister was behind the prank."

He cupped my elbow and guided me out of the way of the group of boys who were headed in our direction.

I shivered, but not in delight, as I shrugged out of his hold.

"Sloane is not my sister. My dad and her mom are kicking it in the bedroom." He waggled his eyebrows, raking his gaze over me.

I seriously needed a shower. "You didn't answer the question."

One of the dark-haired boys in the group flicked his head at Trevor. "Hey, man."

Trevor barely acknowledged him before he regarded me. "Did you ask her?"

"She wouldn't tell me if she did." It was a waste of time to ask Sloane anything. I thought by now the rumor mill would be rife with news of who unleashed my sweet pigs into the school. But no one was talking or whispering or anything. It was like the pig prank had never happened. "I gotta run. Nice chat."

A tall brunette bounced down the hall, gunning for Trevor. Her high ponytail swung like Apple's tail when she was excited to see me.

"Trev, are we on for after school?" She was the girl I'd seen him making out with.

I hurried off, my legs moving as fast as they could.

"Hey, Claire. I'll text you. I've got practice first." Trevor hustled up to my side. "Would you reconsider tutoring me?"

I snorted out a laugh. "What happened to Elise?"

"She's all over the place in her explanation of a function and a theorem. I'm having a hard time. I hear you're the best." His tone was serious, and he sounded desperate.

A pang of guilt zipped through me. Maybe I had him pegged all wrong. Maybe he was just a good guy with a fake bully exterior, or maybe he just wanted attention. "Who told you that?"

"Coach Dean."

I was flattered Coach thought highly of me. He had asked for my opinion on occasion when he needed a teenager's advice about something. "I see."

"He told me to ask you." Trevor said.

Great! The last thing I wanted to do was disappoint Coach. After all, he was Daddy's best bud and Maiken's former coach. "My boyfriend used to play for Coach Dean."

"I heard. I guess Sloane has the hots for your boy's sophomore brother. I don't get it."

I did. Marcus might be an ass, but he was handsome. "Have you met Marcus?" I didn't know when he would have, since Marcus was at the academy with Maiken. Sure, he could've come home, but if Marcus did, then Maiken would too. Unless Marcus was skipping school, which was more of a possibility than anything.

"I have. Kind of a tool if you ask me."

I giggled. Then realized I was laughing with him. *Shame on me.* I didn't exactly get along with Marcus, but I shouldn't be laughing at Maiken's brother.

"That's a pretty sound," Trevor said. "You should laugh more."

I came to an abrupt stop outside the library. "Did you just compliment me?" I asked for nothing more than to convince myself a bully was capable of being nice.

His features pinched. "Why? You don't like compliments?"

I sighed. "In one breath, you're a bully, and in the next, you're nice. I guess I'm not sure if you want me to help you or if you have something else in mind."

His lips curled slightly at the edges. "Something else sounds good, wild one."

I shuddered. His pet name for me made the hairs on my arm stand at attention. "Why are you calling me wild one? It's awful. Don't you have a better pickup line?" Maybe I should give him lessons on manners. "Don't answer that. Why are you behind in your classes?"

He paled and tensed. "Not up for discussion."

"Sorry, Trevor. I don't have time." I pulled open the door and went into the library.

Lo and behold, Trevor followed. When I commandeered a table in the back corner where it was quiet, Trevor joined me, but his body was seemingly too big for the chair.

I huffed. "Can I be honest?"

He snatched his phone out of the front pocket of his jeans. "I love a girl who speaks her mind."

"I literally don't have time. I'm slammed with my own studies and chores on my farm. If I want to keep my valedictorian status, I need to tutor myself."

He slid his phone across the table.

I sat back as though the phone were a weapon. "What are you doing?"

"You want to know why I keep calling you wild one." He pointed at the phone. "Take a look. If I were you, I would turn the sound down."

I studied him, unsure of my next move. Whatever was on his phone couldn't be good, and I'd learned long ago that phones and teenagers spelled all kinds of trouble.

"Go ahead," he said again. "Don't be afraid."

My stomach knotted, and the voice in my head said not to look, but my hands didn't listen. I picked up the phone slowly, holding my breath. When my eyes landed on the screen, nausea shot up and settled in my throat.

"What in the world?" The picture was dark and grainy, but it looked like Maiken and me. I was greedily fumbling with Maiken's belt like I was a hungry animal desperate to eat. "Did you take this video?"

Trevor deadpanned as he crossed bulky arms over his white Henley. Suddenly, that creepy vibe I had about him was stronger than ever.

My pulse banged like a drum solo in a rock concert as I lowered the volume before hitting play. Heat rose like a fast-moving wildfire and gripped my cheeks. I couldn't move. My mouth was bone dry. I couldn't even breathe. I watched in horror as the video unfolded before me. Maiken and I were the stars of the show. *Holy cow!*

Nausea swirled violently in my stomach. If Trevor was speaking, I couldn't hear him over the loud *thump, thump, thump* of my pulse.

The library walls closed in. Nightmares were in my future, and so was hell, or a convent, especially if Daddy found out or saw the video. If this went around school, I couldn't show my face ever again. The words *slut*, *hussy*, and *whore* came to mind. More importantly, something like this could ruin my future employment.

Motherpucker.

Maiken was right. Someone had been watching us the night of my party. He'd thought the person was my dad. I believed Trevor was much more lethal. He could send this video out to the world. I could handle Daddy. Sure, I might be grounded for an eternity, but if Trevor shared the video, I wouldn't be able to attend school without leers, jeers, catcalls, and derogatory name calling. Then again, disappointing Daddy would drive a stake through my heart, and that was way worse than the peer pressure.

Tears were on the brim, ready to spill, but I wasn't about to give Trevor the satisfaction. I stopped the video, tempted to throw his phone at the wall or crush it. That would get rid of any chance he had to send that video to anyone.

Stupid, stupid, stupid girl. Note to self: don't ever drink again.

"Who else has this?" My voice was surprisingly steady when my insides were nothing but.

He leaned forward, showing no expression and no feelings. He was just a clean sheet of paper. "Just me. It's quite sexy. Don't you think?"

He was a pervert.

I gritted my teeth. "Why would you do this?"

His large hands crept across the table before he snagged his phone. "I liked what I saw."

"You're a perv and a bully." My bottom lip wobbled. I was ready to choke and cry and scream. Where was my brother Carter when I needed him? Or Maiken for that matter?

"I haven't shown it to anyone but you," he said as a matter of fact. "I don't plan to either. I'm not like that. Some things should be kept private."

I finally choked. "Private." I hunched over the table. "If you think that, you would've never taken this freaking video." I kept my voice low but hard. Mentally, I was kicking myself in the ass over and over again for my actions. It would've been one thing if a slew of kids hadn't been feet away from Maiken and me that night, although if I hadn't had the party, then I wouldn't have gotten drunk in the first place.

Trevor jutted out his angular jaw. "I was bored and exploring new territory."

Unbelievable.

"Are you using this to bribe me now?" I couldn't wrap my mind around any other reason he would be showing it to me. I didn't want to tutor him, so he had the video to use against me.

Oh my God! If Sloane got ahold of this, I would definitely die.

"Truth, wild one?"

I clenched my fists in my lap, puffing out my cheeks. "Stop calling me that."

"I'm trying to make friends, not enemies." His tone didn't have one threat or an ounce of sarcasm in it. He sounded serious, which was odd since he'd given off the bully vibe.

I laughed loudly, mainly from nerves. The librarian gave me the evil eye from her desk in the distance.

"Why don't I believe you?" Well, a tiny part of me did, but I needed more convincing.

"Quinn," he said in a sweet, husky tone. "I like you. I like you even better since you punched Sloane at your party. I have no ulterior motives here. I'm a guy, and I like porn."

The word "porn" scraped across my arm, and I shivered. Nevertheless, I studied him hard as he held my gaze, steady, unwavering, wanting me to believe him.

Maybe he was an expert liar. There was only one way to test the waters and find out how truthful he was.

I crossed my arms over my chest, willing the contents of my stomach to stay put. "So you'll delete the video, then."

He handed me his phone. "You delete it. That way, you know it's gone, and we start with trusting one another. I've seen better porn anyway."

My jaw hit the table. Maybe I had him pegged all wrong. Still, I wasted no time in wiping that baby off his phone. I deleted it from the trash as well. Once I did, I sighed so darn heavily that the building probably shook.

"Now that we got that out of the way, will you tutor me?" he asked. "Or do I have to tell Coach Dean you said no?"

I shook my head. "Fine. But on one condition."

"Name it."

"We never speak of that video ever again." I couldn't even tell Maiken. Not that I was embarrassed with Maiken, but he might do something stupid as in beat Trevor to a pulp. Then he might ruin his chances of a scholarship or get kicked out of the academy. He might not be as rebellious Marcus, but all the Maxwells had that protective nature when it came to their loved ones.

"What video?" Trevor asked playfully.

That knot in my stomach loosened. I dodged a bullet. Maybe my senior year was looking up after all.

Chapter 16

Maiken

I had been having Quinn withdrawals for weeks. We'd FaceTimed a few nights ago. That had been the best day ever. I kept touching the screen, hoping by some miracle I could actually put my hand through it and feel her soft skin or kiss her sweet lips.

"What are you doing?" she'd asked.

"Trying to touch you," I'd responded.

Then she would giggle.

We'd spent two hours talking and staring at each other. In the end, we'd kissed the screen. That was sort of weird, but I didn't care.

The team had filed out a minute ago while I took a breath and laced up my basketball shoes. My stomach was flipping like a well-practiced gymnast performing her floor routine. The scrimmage game was turning out to be more than practice. The stands were packed. Electricity was in the air, and I felt like I was about to play my first game ever. In part, I was. It would be my first game at the academy. It would also be one where I had to do more than my very best.

Coach Green had invited his good friend Richard Patrick, a scout from Boston College, to the game. He'd sprung that news on the team an hour ago. Between my excitement to see Quinn and now the scout, I was ready to lose my lunch, literally.

Boston College wasn't my first choice, but it was a Division I school. Plus, it was in the NCAA and the ACC conferences, which meant that if I did play for BC, I would go up against Liam at NC State. It would be weird since Liam and I were practically best buds, but it would be fun and cool just the same.

Once my shoes were tied, I opened and closed my fists, trying to keep my hands from shaking. The scout wasn't just in the stands to watch me. Our point guard, Wade, was a great player and graduating with me. He too was interested in a full ride to a Division I school.

I closed my eyes and said a quick prayer, when the door to the locker room squeaked open.

"Maxwell, are you in here?" Coach Green asked before he emerged from behind a bank of lockers. "How come you're not out on the court?" He was dressed in a blue suit and maroon shirt. His suit jacket had the Greenridge Academy's gold insignia stitched on the upper left breast. "Is there a problem?"

I pushed to my feet, tossed my bag in my locker, and closed it. "Not really. Just taking a moment to quiet my nerves."

"Get out there and warm up," he ordered. "That's the best way to shake things off."

"Yes, sir." I headed for the door.

"Maiken, play just like you have been in practice. And remember, this is just a scrimmage."

Scrimmage or not, the game was still the game. I still wanted to win. I still wanted to be perfect whether the scout was in the stands or not.

Coach and I walked out, not saying a word until just before we reached the doorway into the gym. Then he swung out his arm and looked me right in the eye. His dark gaze was resolute. "Get in your zone. Tune everything out but the game. Focus on shooting, rebounds, and passing, exactly like we've been practicing for weeks."

I got the feeling he was trying to calm himself down rather than me. Nevertheless, the buzz of the crowd only enhanced the swirling tornado in my stomach. "I hear Lennox Prep plays dirty. Is that true?" Wade had mentioned that to me earlier.

"They're aggressive," he said. "They have a good defense, as I pointed out in our meeting earlier. We'll be using a man-to-man defense to start the game. They did lose two of their best players last year, so we'll see. But what you need to do is play your game."

I nodded then jogged out and joined my teammates at the other end of the gym, hoping I made him proud.

An hour and twenty minutes later, I was soaked with sweat as the clock ticked down to thirty seconds left in the game. So far, I'd played my game. I'd made Coach proud. Greenridge was in sync. We played like a well-oiled machine, but so did Lennox Prep.

We were down by one point with possession of the ball when Coach Green called a time-out.

The ref blew his whistle.

We huddled around Coach as he started to draw the last play on his clipboard. Up until now, I hadn't had much time to find Quinn in the stands, or the scout for that matter. However, I didn't know what Richard Patrick looked like.

Ian, our power forward, who had been at basketball camp, nudged me. "Hey, there's Noah. Remember the dude at camp?"

Noah? He had called right before I'd moved up to Greenridge that day I was with Quinn at the farm.

I glanced out at the stands across from us. Up until that point, I hadn't dared look at the crowd, mainly to keep my focus on the game. "Where?" I'd returned Noah's call that day, but he hadn't answered, and since then, we hadn't connected.

"Third row up. Left side at the end. He's sitting with a pretty girl."

My gaze shifted in that direction until Coach Green said my name. "Wade, pass to Maiken. Maxwell, we just need a two-pointer to win the game. But use the clock. Understood?"

All of us nodded.

Once we were in position, waiting on the red, I tossed a quick look over my shoulder and froze.

Quinn and Noah were sitting together, bumping shoulders, and laughing. I must've missed a memo somewhere. I'd never told Quinn about Noah. He knew I had a girlfriend, but I hadn't mentioned her name. He hadn't told me much about him, so I hadn't shared much of my history except that I lived in Ashford, had gone to Kensington, and had a girl.

The whistle blew, but I couldn't turn my head.

Wade ran up to me and shouted in my ear. "Dude! Play!"

Fuck.

I shook my head, kicked my legs into gear, and headed down the court.

Coach Green was yelling at the top of his lungs with my name dropping from his angry lips.

I checked the score. We were still down by one. Ian had the ball and passed it to Wade, who, in turn, passed it back to Ian.

I lit a fire under my ass and positioned myself at the side of the key.

"You only need two points," Coach had said.

My pulse soared off the charts. I was so getting my ass reamed.

Wade lined up at the top as I waited for him to look at me. But he didn't. He bounced the ball once and, as if in slow motion, shot the ball.

I held my breath as the ball soared through the air, the seconds ticking by. When the ball hit the backboard, I was sure it wasn't going in. But just as the buzzer went off, the ball fell through the net.

Air punched from my lungs.

The crowd shouted and clapped, and the noise level was off the charts. I swore the building shook. If this was just a scrimmage, I couldn't imagine how the fans would react when we won during the season.

But maybe I wouldn't be there after today to see it. I hung my head as I jogged up to my teammates. "I'm so sorry."

"What happened?" Wade asked, throwing his arms around me.

"I'll tell you later." Right now we had to exchange pleasantries with the other team, and then I had to apologize to Coach.

My stomach was one big knot, because I knew he was going to spit fire over how I'd messed up. *Goodbye to any potential I had with Boston College.*

As I shook the hand of my last opponent, I stole a look at Quinn.

She was studying me hard, and I couldn't quite figure out her expression. It was a cross between confusion and worry.

She smiled tentatively at me, and I returned her gesture. I didn't believe she would dump me for Noah. However, my mind was working overtime, wondering how they knew each other.

They probably just met while sitting in the stands. What I couldn't figure out was why Noah was even at one of my games. Maybe he was enrolling in Greenridge, or he already had, and I just didn't know about it.

What chafed my insides, though, was that Noah and Quinn seemed chummy, as though they knew each other well.

"Maxwell," Coach Green called. "Meet me in my office in five."

I nodded as I joined Wade, who was heading to the locker room.

"What gives?" Wade asked. "You froze, man. Seconds left in the game, and you checked out. Not cool at all."

I hung my head. "It won't happen again." I would make darn sure I didn't even glance at the crowd during the next game, even if Quinn wasn't in the stands. "I saw my girl with someone who I wasn't expecting to see."

"You got to leave the personal shit in the locker room. It has no place on the court." Spoken like a true captain. "You get a pass since this is your first game, and it doesn't count. But when the season starts, your mind better be on the fucking game." He hurried off to catch up with Ian.

I slowed my pace, running my hands through my hair and taking in a deep breath. *Now to talk to Coach.* Instead of showering, I took a left down the hall to Coach's office, where I waited outside.

Within less than a minute, Coach strutted down the hall with his hands tucked into the pockets of his suit pants. He wore a look of pure disappointment. "What happened?" His voice boomed in the empty hall.

I swallowed an elephant, afraid to tell him what I'd just told Wade. But I wasn't one to lie. "I saw my girl. That's all."

He pointed at me, and it was the first time I'd seen him angry. "If you pull something like that again, I will bench you for five games." His tone brooked no argument. "Do I make myself clear?"

A shiver of fear danced up my spine as I nodded in rapid succession. "Yes, sir."

The last thing I wanted to do was disappoint him. He'd gone out of his way for me since I'd arrived at the school. He'd counseled me. He'd checked on me. He'd treated me like the son he never had. I only knew the latter because he'd told me that very thing. He and his wife had tried to have a boy, but after three tries and three girls, they'd decided their family was big enough.

"Hit the shower."

I started to leave then stopped. "Coach? Do you think I messed up any chance with the BC scout?"

He grabbed the door handle to his office. "You need to worry about the next game and not freezing up." Then he went inside.

Several cuss words zipped around in my head. I wasn't mad at anyone but myself.

Chapter 17

Quinn

"What is taking him so long?" I paced the white-and-gray hardwood in the gym.

Celia wanted to roam the school since this was her first time at the academy. "I've heard a few things over the years about this school," she'd said on the car ride up. "Tough, cliquey, and lots of drama."

Most high schools were exactly that. Kensington wasn't any different.

My response had been, "You left out bullies."

Noah was absorbed in his phone. Celia was too.

Marcus, Jasper, Emma, and Ethan had left as soon as the game was done, although Emma promised she would be back to catch up with Celia and me before we left. But I knew the truth. She'd run back to her dorm to fix her hair and dab on some makeup to impress Noah. She had been smitten with him since he'd sat down next to me

"Maiken is probably getting his ass chewed," Noah said. "He froze."

It was my fault. He probably thought Noah was trying to move in on me.

"Tell me more about basketball camp. You roomed with Maiken? How come I'm just now learning about this? Did you know he and I were dating?"

Celia looked up from her phone. "Yeah. Did you know they were dating?"

Noah gnawed on the inside of his cheek. "I tried to get ahold of Maiken when I found out my mom took a job in Ashford, but we never connected. He'd never mentioned your name. We didn't talk about family. I don't like the subject, frankly."

Celia and I had both been surprised to see him sitting in the stands. At first, I'd thought I was at Kensington until my gaze had landed on Greenridge's state championship banners hanging from the rafters.

A door creaked open, causing my gaze to dart to the far end of the gym. My heart nearly jumped out of my chest.

Maiken's muscular thighs, encased in dark jeans, ate up the space between us as he beelined it for me, unleashing a belly-tingling grin.

I kicked my feet into gear, and then I was running full-out, like I was sprinting to the finish line.

Stopping, he braced his legs, knowing what was about to happen. I didn't want us tumbling to the floor, at least not on the hard surface. It would hurt his back, and he'd already had problems with his lower spine.

His lips split into an even bigger grin. "I got you, babe."

Goose bumps exploded on my body, and fireworks went off in my head as I leapt into his arms.

He laughed, wild and free, as his hands went into my hair. "I've missed you."

I peppered kisses along his ear. "I was dying to run out on the court when you were playing." I squeezed him as tightly as I could. If we stayed like this the rest of the night, I was okay with that.

He gripped my waist and helped me down on two feet. Then he planted his lips on mine softly and tentatively. "I'm afraid if I kiss you, I won't let go."

That wasn't a bad thing. So I gave him a nudge and darted out my tongue. He didn't hesitate, kissing me hungrily and greedily as though it would be our last kiss for a long time.

In essence, it was.

He tasted sweet and minty, making me whimper.

"You two should really get a room," Noah said at my back.

"I agree," Celia added.

"A room alone with you sounds amazing," Maiken said as he nibbled on my lip.

Reluctantly, I began to pry myself from him until he whispered in my ear. "Give me a minute before you turn around."

I didn't have to ask why. I could feel his excitement for me. I needed to distract him. So I asked, "Did you get in trouble?"

He blew out a breath. "Not really." Then he nodded, giving me the go-ahead that I could turn and face my BFF and Noah.

Noah was staring at Maiken as though he were trying to read him. "Good game, bro." He stepped closer to Maiken, and the two exchanged a bro hug.

Celia flicked her dark hair off her shoulder. "Maiken, long time, no see."

Maiken raked his blue gaze over Celia. "You look good after that fall at Quinn's party."

"I have a hard head," Celia teased.

"Did you three just meet tonight at the game?" Maiken asked evenly despite the hard vibe jumping off him and onto Noah.

The four of us stood in a circle of sorts, and I slipped my hand into Maiken's. I wanted to feel him as much as I could before Celia and I headed home in a couple of hours. Daddy had been adamant that we get on the road early. He didn't want us driving back in the dead of night.

"He goes to Kensington," Celia said.

One part confusion and one part shock washed over Maiken. "Really?"

Noah held up his big hands. "I called you. You were supposed to call me back and never did."

"I left you a voice mail," Maiken volleyed in return.

I squeezed his hand. "I just learned tonight he was your roomie at camp."

Celia slipped her phone in her purse. "Did you know Dustin Lane and Noah are cousins?"

Maiken glared at his friend. "For real?"

Sensing or reading Maiken's stiff body language, Noah said, "My mom took a job in Ashford, and just before she did, she told me about a step-cousin I never knew I had. I called you that day to tell you the news."

I wagged a finger between the boys. "You really didn't share much at camp, huh?"

Noah laughed. "Nah. I didn't tell Maiken squat about me except that I move a lot. And he didn't share much either except that he had a girlfriend and lived in Ashford. I have a dysfunctional, screwed-up family I don't like talking about. Nothing is going on here, bro, if that's what you're thinking." He stabbed a finger at me while keeping his gaze locked on Maiken's. "Full disclosure, though. I did try to ween in on Quinn until I found out the first week from the basketball team that you two were dating. Then I backed off."

"I was curious why you stopped hounding Quinn," Celia said, echoing what I was thinking.

Maiken draped an arm over my shoulder and pulled me to him as though he were making sure Noah knew he wasn't getting anywhere near me.

A second of thick, soupy silence stretched between them.

"You came up to see me play, then?" Maiken asked.

Noah beamed. "Dude, I've been trying to convince my mom to send me here. She gave me the thumbs-up to check out the place. And I heard from Coach Dean that you were playing tonight. So two birds, one stone, and all that."

Maiken lit up. And just like that, any animosity was gone as though someone had stuck a pin into a balloon and popped the air out of it. "Wow! That would be awesome."

I tugged on his hand. "Can you wrap this up?" Not that I was bored, since I was glued to Maiken's side. "I would like to spend time with my boyfriend before we get on the road."

Maiken kissed me on my temple. "Want to take a walk?"

I wanted to do anything other than stand there.

"Quinn. Celia." Emma's voice echoed in the humungous room as she bounced up, her ponytail swishing behind her. "We didn't get to meet earlier." Her big brown eyes were on Noah. "I'm Emma, Maiken's sister."

Noah tensed. Maiken did as well.

Celia and I exchanged a knowing smile.

Poor Noah. He was sort of screwed. He couldn't date me. He couldn't date Emma either because of the bro code. However, Celia wasn't off limits. She liked Noah, but she was digging Sloane's brother, Trevor, more. But Trevor had his lips on the brunette, Claire, and seemed to be into her more than any other girl.

Still, I could see the attraction. Where Noah was tall and lanky, Trevor was tall and beefy. Celia liked beefy.

I was warming up to Trevor. Under all his bully layers and mean comments, he was just a boy who was looking for attention, much like Sloane and Marcus.

"Why don't we head down to the pizza place on campus?" Emma asked.

Celia's lips parted. "There's a pizza restaurant on campus? I want to go to this school. Maybe I'll talk to my mom too."

"I don't think so," I rushed out. "My BFF isn't leaving me."

She snorted. "We should convince your dad, then."

As much as I would like to see Maiken every day, that wasn't happening. My parents wouldn't let me go to another high school. Besides, they didn't have the money to send me to a rich academy. "Good luck with that."

Maiken's lips grazed my ear. "I would love that. We could snuggle up in your dorm room or mine."

I shivered in delight. "Maybe college."

Emma hooked her arm in Noah's. "Enough talk. Let's get something to eat."

Maiken growled low.

Noah chuckled as if to tell Maiken he didn't have anything to worry about when it came to Emma. But if I knew strong-willed Emma, Maiken didn't stand a chance of telling her who she could or couldn't date.

Celia looped her arm around Noah's free one. "I'm starving."

"We'll catch up," Maiken said.

Once we were alone, Maiken's lips crashed to mine. His tongue dove in hard and fast like he was a starving boy. I wasn't complaining. I'd been dying to kiss him for what felt like forever.

But he broke away before I could get lost in us. "Come on. I want to show you something."

I pouted, licking his minty taste off my lips.

He gave me a wolfish grin. "I promise you'll love what I have to show you."

Five minutes later, we were two lovers, holding hands, strolling the rolling hills of the academy under the stars, where nothing mattered but him and me. The scene was romantic, serene, thrilling, and I felt like I was on cloud nine. Something between us seemed to be stronger, more powerful. Maybe it was because we didn't see each other every day, and the separation was heightening my emotions.

My feet sank into the plush grass as the moonlight guided us. "Where are we going?"

"Somewhere quiet where it's just you and me."

I squeezed his hand. "I like that plan. I miss our time in the supply closet at school."

He chuckled. "Where I'm taking you is ten times better than a closet."

I didn't care where we ended up as long as I was with him.

The academy grew distant behind us as we trudged across the expanse of the property for another five minutes. Finally, Maiken settled near a large oak tree. Then he bent down, cleared away a pile of fallen leaves, and picked up a blanket.

My eyes widened. "Planning ahead?"

He grinned. "For sure. I thought this would be a great place to lay under the stars." He looked up. "On a clear night, like tonight, the sky is amazing."

I glanced skyward, and he was right. The stars twinkled and shined like I'd never seen them do before. I thought the view from my farm was pretty spectacular, but it was nothing compared to this. Where we were, nestled in the Berkshires with dense trees surrounding the property, I felt like I was on another planet.

I snagged the blanket from him and shook it out before I placed it on the ground. "It's beautiful up here."

He tugged me to him. "You're beautiful."

I threw my arms around him and kissed him with every ounce of energy I had.

He chuckled, a sound that made me break out in goose bumps as he pulled me down onto the blanket. "I've missed you."

"Shhh. No talking. Just kissing."

Maiken tasted sweet, minty, and delicious.

He adjusted us so he was on top with his hands on each side of my head. "I just want to look at you for a minute. You're beautiful, Quinn Thompson. You're my starlight. You shine like an angel, and I love you hard."

I flattened my hands on his jaw. "And you are the best thing that has ever happened to me."

His blue gaze searched mine. "Your butterscotch hair shimmers in the moonlight."

I beamed up at him, my heart swooning and my body tingling. "Your poem." He'd written me a couple of them during the last year or so.

He nibbled on my bottom lip. "Your amber eyes sparkle and ignite." His tongue darted into my mouth. "Mmm... Your lips... are soft and taste like berry."

I couldn't help but smile. "Nothing about our relationship is temporary," I said, reciting his next line.

He moved a strand of hair from my eyes. "And when I look at you like you hung the moon, all I do is swoon and swoon and swoon."

Tears of happiness and content and so much more surfaced. "I love you to the stars and back, Maiken Maxwell."

He cemented his mouth to mine, kissing, taking, possessing. I was the happiest girl around as I matched him kiss for kiss and tongue for tongue.

This boy had my heart in the palm of his hand.

Chapter 18

Quinn

While I waited for Trevor to show up, I reminisced, staring off into space. It had been five days since I'd seen Maiken at the academy. Five days since we'd held hands and strolled the grounds in the moonlight and kissed until our lips were swollen. That night under the stars had been amazing and one of the best times of my life. It felt like we had grown so much closer.

The door to the library creaked open, sounding ominous in the quiet space, and pulling me back to the present. I blinked a few times as I scanned the room. A handful of kids sat at tables scattered around, with their heads buried in books.

Trevor and I had agreed to meet on Wednesdays right after lunch since we both had a free period. The time worked out perfectly. He had basketball practice after school, and I had to get home on most days to get my chores done.

But the person gliding around tables liked she owned the damn library was none other than Sloane Price. Her hair was pulled back off her forehead. Her big brown eyes were heavily made up in a smoky look with blue eye shadow and a ton of mascara. Her solid black outfit brought out the white-blond color of her hair, and she was eyeing me as though she had a bone to pick.

Great!

She settled across the table, not sitting down. "Quinn." Her voice was light, belying the petty snarl she had going on. "I hear you're tutoring my stepbrother."

I set my phone down, Maiken's poem fading from my memory. *Argh!* I was having a perfectly good week. I was ready for my test in calculus that afternoon, and I was still riding on a love high since seeing Maiken. He and I had been texting more than ever, and even though he wasn't in school with me, I kind of felt like we had a secret love affair going on. I knew that sounded ditzy, but I had to make the best of our separation. Not only that, but Thanksgiving was three weeks out, and he was coming home.

"You heard correctly."

She flattened her red lips together as though she were holding back from yelling at me. "Don't. Stay as far away from him as possible."

I sat back. She was a confusing individual—nice one minute, a witch the next. She'd been through a rough time. She blamed herself for her father's death. I couldn't begin to know how that felt, and I hoped and prayed I never would.

"Are you worried about me?" I didn't see any emotion in her brown eyes.

"We've had our differences, but I don't want to see you get hurt."

"Um, I'm only tutoring him. I need the gig for my college apps."

She scanned the library like she had a big secret. Then she leaned over the table. "Just be careful. Trevor is an asshole."

He had that quality about him, so I couldn't exactly disagree. Still, he hadn't been a jerk to me since I'd deleted the video from his phone.

"He's got a girlfriend. Right?"

Disgust filled Sloane's eyes. "Please tell me you're not interested in him."

I knitted my brow. "For real? Hello? Maiken Maxwell. My point is, if he has a girlfriend, then he's not interested in me. Besides, he gave me the impression he needs to get his grades up to play ball."

She lost her attitude. "Well, that is true. His dad has been cracking the whip with him and his grades."

"See? Nothing to worry about." Not that it was any of my business, but I had to ask. "Why didn't you move like you were supposed to?"

"My mom's job offer fell through. At least that's what she tells me. But it was around the same time she met Trevor's dad. I'm not even sure why I'm spilling all this to you."

Again, she was a confusing person. "I don't know either. Don't take this the wrong way, but you're moody. One day, you're nice to me, and the next, you treat me like I stabbed you with a knife. What gives? And why were you such a bitch to me at my party?"

Before then, I hadn't done anything to get on her bad side.

"Sorry about that. I was having a bad day." She seemed like she meant it.

"I'm sorry too." I regretted a lot of things about that night, like drinking.

"What are you two talking about?" Trevor asked, coming up behind Sloane.

I hadn't seen him walk into the library. For all I knew, he could've been lurking in between the bookshelves.

He hung his arm over Sloane's shoulder. "Sis, are you getting tutored too?" His tone was sickly sweet with a dash of salt.

Sloane went ramrod straight as she sneered. "I got to study for a test." Without so much as a goodbye, she dashed away to a table on the other side of the library as though Trevor had the plague.

He set his backpack down then dragged a chair closer to me.

"You don't have to sit so close."

"I do, Quinn. I can't read upside down. Besides, you smell good."

I rolled my eyes. "I'm not interested."

"Too bad. I make good boyfriend material."

Not as good as Maiken. "Let's get started. We only have forty minutes now since you're late. If you want my help, be on time."

Flicking blond strands of hair out of his eyes, he pulled out his algebra book from his bag. "I had something to do."

"Nothing is more important than your grades. Right?" If he wasn't serious, then I was wasting my time.

"Yes, teach."

"Good. Now open your book to chapter five. I think that's where we left off." I sounded like one of my teachers when she was frustrated with a student.

Just as we were about to start, a brunette sashayed up. If I wasn't mistaken, this was Claire. I wasn't used to seeing her without her lips suctioned to Trevor's.

I growled under my breath.

"Trev, babe, you forgot this." She dropped a black thong on the table with a coy smile.

Trevor didn't blush or react. He grabbed the lacy undergarment and tucked it in his back pocket as I gaped at him. *Disgusting.* But then again, he had taken a video of Maiken and me in a compromising position, so I shouldn't be surprised.

Claire came around the table, leaned into Trevor's ear, and whispered something I couldn't make out.

Trevor snaked his arm around one of her thighs. "Claire, I have work to do. We'll pick up where we left off later tonight."

She kissed him on the cheek. "Counting on it."

I rolled my eyes as she wiggled her hips and blew a kiss over her shoulder at Trevor.

"You're late because you got a quickie?" I mumbled. "Unbelievable. Maybe this was a mistake."

He grabbed my wrist. "Don't go. I promise I won't be late again."

"It doesn't sound like you're as serious as you were the other day. Are you jerking me around?"

His green eyes darkened. "Is that what Sloane put in your head?"

"Sloane didn't have to put anything in my head. I have my own studying to do, and I am not wasting my time with an asshole."

He slapped a hand over his heart. "I'm hurt."

I shook my head, ready to pack up. Anger fired through every nerve ending. Maybe Sloane was right for me to stay away from Trevor.

"Quinn." His tone was soft and sweet. "I'm sorry."

I huffed. "Time is precious to me, Trevor. I only have a small window to help you. I barely have time to do my own homework. With my brothers away at college, I'm the only one to help my dad on the farm. Maybe you should go back to Elise for tutoring."

"Please," he said, batting his eyelashes. "Give me a chance."

I held up my finger. "One. And no girls at the table, interrupting us. Got it?"

He saluted me. "Yes, commander."

I half smiled as we dove into algebra.

Chapter 19

Maiken

The words on the page were fuzzy. I couldn't read or study anymore. I closed my US government book. Politics wasn't my thing. But it was either that elective or psychology, and US government seemed like it would be easier.

Knuckles rapped on the door.

"Yeah, it's open."

Marcus strutted in, wearing a pair of sweatpants and nothing else. He glanced at Ethan's bed. "It's almost curfew."

I traded my desk chair for my bed. "Says the guy who almost always misses curfew."

The day Jasper had told Ethan and me that Marcus had gone to Ashford, none of us thought he would make it back before lights out. To our surprise, he had. Since then, he hadn't seen Sloane or gone back to Ashford, at least not to my knowledge.

"Ethan is working out. He should be back shortly."

Marcus sat on the edge of Ethan's bed. "I have something to tell you, and I don't want you to get upset."

On that note, my pulse sped up. "You're running away with Sloane," I teased. But deep down, I wasn't. I wanted Marcus to be happy, and if Sloane was the gal to give him a purpose in life, then so be it. I couldn't talk anyway. Marcus wasn't enamored with Quinn, but he didn't ride my ass about her, although I wasn't drinking and acting out or running back to Ashford.

Marcus regarded me, his blue eyes steady and piercing. He and I were the only two out of the eight of us siblings who had blue eyes. However, he'd come out with brown hair rather than the sandy blond I had.

"Well, are you going to stare at me or tell me what's on your mind? If it is Sloane, man, I'm cool."

His lips curled, barely smiling. "You mean you're okay with us dating again?"

I scooted up so my back was resting against the headboard. "Yeah."

"We're not exactly." He picked at a nail. "We're trying the whole friends thing."

I cocked my head. "Why would that make me upset?"

"This is not about Sloane and me." He took a deep breath. "I told you about Sloane's stepbrother."

He had when he'd returned from Ashford that day. Marcus had instantly hated the guy. Apparently, Sloane didn't like how a stranger had waltzed into her life and her mother's.

But her stepbrother wasn't my problem. "He's a dick. So?"

"Have you talked to Quinn lately?"

I held the air in my lungs, nodding. "Why?"

"Sloane is worried about her."

A laugh rumbled free. "Sloane? The girl who doesn't like Quinn?"

"That's not the point," Marcus said. "Quinn is tutoring Trevor. Sloane gets the impression he's up to something with her."

Quinn had told me she'd decided not to tutor him. I wondered if Principal Sanders had forced Quinn's hand. "Like?"

"I don't know. Neither does Sloane."

Ethan waltzed in, sweaty and looking upset. He tore his T-shirt off and tossed it in the corner with the rest of his dirty clothes.

"What's up your ass?" Marcus asked.

He grabbed his shower gear. "Jessica. She won't stop texting and calling me."

Marcus arched a brow. "I thought you liked her."

I hopped off my bed. "I'll let you two figure out girls. I need to call Quinn." I also needed a private spot.

I inhaled the brisk night air two minutes later as I held the phone to my ear, waiting for Quinn to answer.

The grounds of the academy were desolate as curfew approached. The landscape lighting glowed along the path as I walked down toward the football field.

"Everything okay?" Quinn answered, sounding like she was yawning.

"I just wanted to hear your voice before I crashed for the night." That was mostly true.

"Aw, I love you too. I was about to go to bed. It's been a tense day."

My blood gelled. "Something happen?"

"Not exactly. Tests, studying, chores, tutoring. You name it. Oh, and I... Never mind."

I settled along the perimeter of the football field. The moonlight provided an ominous feeling, like the calm before the storm. "Quinn? Did Trevor do something to you?"

She sucked in a breath. "What? Trevor? Why would you ask me that?"

"Marcus came to me earlier. Sloane is worried about you helping him."

"Oh my God. Seriously? Trevor is a nice guy. He needs to get his grades up."

I scraped a hand through my hair. "I thought you didn't want to work with him?"

"Coach Dean wants me to help him. Although I don't think Trevor's girl, Claire, wants me anywhere near him. She won't leave us alone when we're in the library. The other day, she dropped her thong on the table." She giggled. "And Trevor took them and put them in his pocket."

I rolled my eyes, even though she couldn't see me. "How long have you been working with him?"

"A couple of weeks. Maiken, don't worry, babe. It's just tutoring."

I trusted Quinn implicitly. However, I didn't share her sentiment that Trevor was a nice guy. "Didn't you tell me he gave you the creeps?"

She let out a breath. "Yeah, but I think I had him pegged all wrong. I think he was looking for attention."

"Baby doll, I won't hesitate to come home if he so much as tries anything." I made a mental note to call Noah when I hung up with Quinn. He could keep an eye out since both of them played on the basketball team.

"Trevor isn't going to do any such thing. I should get some sleep. Four a.m. comes super fast."

"Before you go, you were about to tell me something."

"It's a surprise." The sound of water running droned in the background.

Surprises weren't my thing, but I couldn't help but grin as butterflies came alive in my stomach. "What's the occasion?" It wasn't my birthday.

"I'll tell you when you come home." I could hear the smile in her voice.

I wasn't sure I could wait another week for Thanksgiving break.

"I'm going to go before I ruin the surprise." I could hear the smile in her voice.

"You know if I were there, I would tickle it out of you."

"Ha. You could try," she teased. "I love you to the stars and back."

"Quinn, dream about me."

"Always. Talk to you tomorrow." Then she hung up.

Man, I was the luckiest guy on earth to have Quinn as my girl. Grinning like the lovestruck dude that I was, I called Noah.

"Hey, man," Noah said. "Something wrong?"

"I need your help. Tell me all about Trevor, Sloane's stepbrother."

"Jeez, nothing to tell really. He's a good ballplayer. Girls drool over him."

"Does Quinn?" I held my breath.

One beat passed, then two, and still no response.

My body was turning numb. I swore that if he so much as said yes, I was hitching a ride to Ashford tonight. "Noah, man, you still there?"

He cleared his throat. "Do you want it straight?"

I belted out a laugh, albeit not a happy one. "No, lie to me. Of course, man."

"He talks about her quite a bit. He definitely has a thing for her. But dude, I did too when I first met her."

I growled. "Fuck."

"Chill," he said calmly. "Quinn is not interested in him, or any guy for that matter. I know. She pushed me away. Hard too."

"She's not tutoring you, though."

"Do you need me to keep an eye out?" he asked.

"Would you?" I hated to spy on her, but if Sloane was worried and felt the need to have Marcus talk to me, then I had to at least heed the warning.

"Consider it done. Hey, on another note, my mom gave me the thumbs-up if I wanted to attend the academy. I thought a lot about it and decided I'm staying at Kensington. I'm just getting to know my cousin Dustin, and I really like playing for Coach Dean, although I think he might be stepping down next year, and your cousin Kade might be taking his spot."

Coach had been noodling on retiring when I played for him, and Kade had stepped in when Coach's wife had gone through some medical issues. I was kind of surprised Coach hadn't retired after last year.

"You'll like Kade."

"I already do. Cool-as-shit guy."

"Agreed. I gotta run. Curfew and all. I'll see you when I come home for Thanksgiving. Call me if Trevor tries anything with Quinn." I ended the call, feeling like a schmuck for spying on my girl.

Chapter 20

Quinn

I bit a nail as I sat on an exam table in the gynecologist's office. I couldn't believe I'd almost spilled the surprise to Maiken on the phone the night before. I'd been dying to tell him I was planning on talking to Momma about going on the pill. I'd finally drummed up the courage to have that conversation with her last week.

She'd been surprised I'd waited so long to talk to her. She had expected me to ask her before school let out my junior year. Nevertheless, she'd made the appointment the very next day.

Mom sat idle on the only chair in the room, deep in thought.

My phone pinged with a text.

Celia: *Well, did you get the pill yet?*

Me: *I'm waiting on the doctor.*

Celia: *Cool. I talked to my mom too. She's going to make an appointment for me.*

Me: *Yay. I better go. We'll talk later.*

Celia: *Trevor is looking for you. He told me to tell you he has to cancel his session with you. He's got to take care of something. He didn't say what, though.*

Me: *Okay.*

Whatever he had to do was none of my business. I did wonder, though, as I set the phone in my lap. He'd been worried about his upcoming exam next week in algebra. If he passed, then that would give him the credits he needed to advance to Geometry and become an official junior.

Mom smoothed a hand over her chestnut hair. "Everything okay?"

"Trevor canceled his session with me."

"You look worried," she said.

"Nah. He has an important test coming up. I just want to see him do well." If he did, then I would feel validated that my time and effort had been worth it. Plus, I really enjoyed tutoring. "Momma, I think I want to change my major from doctor to teacher."

"Why the change?"

I shrugged. "I like teaching." Trevor had been very astute in learning. He'd done his homework. He'd passed the short quizzes I'd given him. He'd even passed his test in his algebra class. I enjoyed explaining things and then seeing how the light bulb came on with my student.

"You've always liked school. I can see you as a great teacher. You would also make a great doctor."

"It might be easier for me to get into a teaching program rather than premed."

She rose elegantly, brushing her hands down her pant legs. "By easier, do you mean cheaper?"

"I would be up to my ears in student loans if I didn't get a scholarship. And even if I did get a scholarship, that wouldn't last. Premed, then medical school, then an internship." I blew out a breath. "I don't know."

"Well, you don't have to decide right this minute. And you're not filling out applications until after the holidays. Right?"

That was the plan. But if I wanted to switch to teaching, then I had to rethink my options for colleges. I resumed biting a nail.

Momma wrapped her delicate fingers around my wrist. "You won't have any nails left."

I didn't anyway. Farm work didn't allow me to have those gel nails that most of the girls in school had on a frequent basis. I would break one in a hot minute for sure.

I placed my hands in my lap. "You didn't tell Daddy what we were doing today, did you?" College options could wait for the time being.

Her brown eyes went wide as she resumed her seat. "It's not a good time to tell him that his baby girl is about to lose her virginity."

I swallowed a clump of mud and cringed at the thought of how Daddy would react. He would probably have a heart attack. "Please don't tell him until I leave for college... or never."

"I don't plan on sharing this with him anytime soon." She tucked my hair behind my ear. "You're such a beautiful girl." The sadness washing over her matched the tone in her voice.

A stabbing pain gripped my heart at the notion of Momma alone in the house without her kids. She was having a hard time with Liam and Carter being in college. I'd overheard her and Daddy talking the other night about their plans for the farm when I left. Daddy didn't have an answer for what he would do or if he would start to downsize and not have as many animals. Momma had suggested he hire two or three ranch hands in preparation for when I went off to school.

Daddy wasn't hearing it, though. He'd promised Momma he would find someone at least for the holidays to work the farm and help sell Christmas trees.

She wiped a tear from my face. "Honey, where did you go?"

I blinked, and another tear fell. "It's been a rough year. Is Daddy going to hire someone?"

"You heard us talking the other night?"

I nodded. "I'm worried about you guys. When I leave, Daddy won't have any help." Celia's suggestion of posting the job on the school's bulletin board came to mind. I decided I would do just that later today if, for no other reason, than to get help for the holidays. Carter and Liam were due home for Thanksgiving, but that was only for a few days. The Christmas tree business started hopping the day after Thanksgiving and stayed busy until at least a week before Christmas.

Momma shifted her gaze back and forth over me. "You have a beautiful soul. You let your father and me worry about the farm."

That was easier said than done. While I could, I would help Daddy find someone. That was the least I could do.

She tipped up my chin. "I'm so proud of you for coming to me." Her chest heaved. "Does Maiken know?"

I shook my head vigorously. "Not yet." I was sure he would be excited, though. "Momma, will it hurt?" I whispered.

She gave me a weak smile. "It will, but if you take it slow, the pain doesn't last long."

I was certain Maiken would be as gentle as possible.

She squeezed my hands, shuddering. "Your father was my first. He's the only man I've ever been with. Are you sure you don't want to wait until you're married?"

I bit my lip. "Did you and Dad?"

She laughed, tapping my nose. "No. But I had to ask, because I can hear your father now. 'They should wait until they're married.'"

I snorted. "For sure. He'll have a cow if he finds out, Momma. Please don't tell him." I couldn't face him if she did. I definitely would turn a million shades of red. Or better yet, I would run away.

"I don't like keeping things from your father. But this is one we can put on the back burner unless he asks."

"Has he asked?" *Please say no.*

She nodded. "He has."

I closed my eyes for a solid ten seconds, willing the pounding of my pulse to ease. "When?" Suddenly, the video that Trevor had filmed of Maiken and me popped into my brain.

"Something wrong?" Momma asked.

I had no reason to worry since the video was gone. "Not at all."

"Quinn Thompson, what are you not telling me?" Momma always knew when her kids lied. "Did you lie to me? Did you have sex?"

"No, ma'am," I said low. "I didn't lie. I promise. It's just that I think I would hide forever if Daddy found out that I'm about to lose my virginity." I couldn't bring myself to tell her about the video. It was a moot point anyway.

Her shoulders sagged as the mixture of fear and anger vanished. "I can understand that."

"Momma, I know this is hard for you. It's equally hard for me, and a bit scary. But I love Maiken. I want him to be the one, and I'm ready. I'll be fine."

I truly would be. I felt better just knowing I was taking measures to protect myself and Maiken and our future. Maybe now I wouldn't be so nervous to allow nature to take its course when Maiken and I were together.

Chapter 21
Quinn

I rubbed my eyes as I walked into the brightly lit kitchen, which was too blinding for four in the morning. The scent of coffee hung heavy in the air as Momma poured herself a cup. I didn't drink the stuff as much as she and Daddy did.

"What are you doing up so early?" I asked.

Normally, Momma slept in an hour longer than Daddy and me. Then she got breakfast started.

She set the carafe back on the burner. "I couldn't sleep. I think I'm coming down with something."

She didn't look pale. "You should go back to bed, then."

"Who's the mom in this house?" she teased. "I have a lot to do anyway. I'm stocking shelves in the store this morning. I wanted to get a head start. We have a ton of orders to fill for Thanksgiving this week."

I grabbed my coat off the rack near the back door. "Momma, are you worried about Maiken and me?" She'd been different since my exam, quieter and more contemplative.

I had a feeling Maiken and I were on her mind since he was home for the holiday. I hadn't planned on taking our relationship to the next level that week. I had too much to do, especially with three more days of school before we were out for the long Thanksgiving weekend.

She cinched her robe tightly. "No, honey. I'm just tired. But speaking of your relationship with Maiken, how are you doing on the pill? Any side effects?"

"None." I'd only been on it a week. So far, I hadn't had any of the bloating or weight gain or anything else the doctor had mentioned.

She picked up her coffee cup. "Good. Your dad is down in the horse barn. I think he hired someone to help out."

My eyebrows lifted. "That would be good." *Really good.* Maybe then I could take a breather or get up an hour later. "Is that person starting today?" I had tacked a job posting to the board in school, so maybe it was someone I knew.

Momma closed the distance between us and kissed me on the forehead. "Not sure. Now go before your father comes screaming for you."

I bundled up, hoping he'd hired a massive guy who could lift things and pick up the slack. Although not many kids at school matched that description. Then I remembered Sloane. She'd applied for a job on the farm last year. Surely she wouldn't again.

Nevertheless, I practically skipped down toward the barn, a cold wind slapping me in the face and waking me up just a tad more.

The spotlight outside the barn came on when I approached. Daddy had installed not only spotlights but cameras too. We still hadn't found out who had used our pigs for the prank at school, but Daddy was ready if the guilty party tried again.

Apple nickered when I entered. "Daddy." I grabbed a pair of work gloves off the table next to the door. "Daddy," I called again, glancing down the stretch of space in between the horse stalls.

I didn't see him, but maybe he was cleaning out a stall. If he were, though, he would have the bales of hay stacked outside, ready to go.

Maybe Momma meant he was in the other barn, where the cows were. He did usually start his morning milking the cows.

I ambled up to Apple to say a quick good morning. "Hey, girl. Maybe we'll go out later before the storm rolls in." Five inches of snow was in the forecast. Apple loved the snow. I loved riding in it too. There was nothing like galloping through the woods while snow fell. "You haven't seen your grandpa anywhere?"

She nuzzled my hand as if to say no.

"Okay, I'll be back to take care of you. I have to feed the pigs first." My chores began with my lovely pigs.

Beast came up to me as soon as I entered the pen two minutes later. "Hey, boy. Smile for the camera." I pointed to a camera up on the corner of the overhang. I dared anyone to take Beast, Godfrey, Lola, or any of the other pigs we had now.

Beast grunted as he pushed his snout into my leg.

"It's good to see you too. Let's get you fed."

As I began feeding the pigs, a big, fat snowflake fell onto my nose then another. A thread of excitement stirred. I knew it was too soon to cancel school, but if the snow did pile up, then school would be let out early, which meant I could see Maiken sooner.

I envied him right then. He was sleeping in a warm bed and dreaming. I couldn't remember a day when I was able to sleep in. Instead, I was up every morning, walking in mud and pig slop, shoveling horse poop, and doing everything else that came with living on a farm. I loved my animals. I loved my parents and growing up on a farm, but it would be nice to have a day off.

Maybe I could sleep in when Carter and Liam came home for the holiday.

So many good things were happening. Daddy hired someone. Maiken was home. And my brothers would be too, which meant fewer chores for me.

Once the pigs were eating and happy, I headed toward the gate, but I didn't see the bucket until it was too late. My arms flew outward, gravity took over, and I was falling backward. I squealed like one of my dear pigs as my butt hit the mud first, then my back and head hit with a thud.

Motherpucker.

Beast came up to me, and his wet nose tickled my ear as he sniffed me. I laughed as the snow fell, and more pigs joined Beast in the fun.

Oh my word. It would take years to get the stench out of my hair. Manure was definitely not the right pheromone to lure Maiken to me.

Sighing heavily, I was about to get up when a tall figure loomed over me.

The man angled his head. His green eyes were like two high beams in the early morning light. "Do you always fall in shit?"

I glared at the boy who was wearing a ball cap and dressed like he'd come to work his tail off in boots, gloves, and even a flannel shirt. "Are you the one my dad hired?"

Trevor grabbed my hand and pulled me up. "The one and only."

"For real? You want to work on a farm?" I wasn't shocked Daddy had hired him. Trevor certainly had the muscle to do the heavy lifting around the farm, something Daddy needed desperately. I was, however, miffed as to why a clean-cut boy who didn't have a callus on his hands wanted to work on a farm.

"I need the money. I saw the flyer at school, and I decided to check it out."

My Spidey sense was screaming at me for some reason. Yet so far, Trevor had shown me nothing but niceness and respect.

He stabbed his thumb in the direction of the horses. "Your dad wants me to start cleaning out the horse stalls. He's going to meet me in the barn."

Daddy and I needed to chat. The way Momma had talked, I thought Daddy would hire someone who would be permanent, as in someone who would stay years, not months.

Trevor took long strides, leaving me standing in shock.

I shook off the mud, or tried to. It was useless to clean the muck out of my hair or off my body since I still had chores. So I wiped my hands on my jeans, not caring that the pig stench was making me a little queasy.

I jogged up to Trevor. "Where have you been? You missed our session last week, and I haven't seen you in school."

"My old man had some business out of town, and he wanted me to go with."

"Your final exam is this week in algebra. Right? Are you ready?"

"I will be. Can we meet after school? I don't have basketball practice this week."

I had plans with Maiken. "Why can't we meet at our usual time after lunch?"

"Mrs. Flowers wants to meet with me."

Our guidance counselor had returned a few weeks prior. I needed to talk to her myself and discuss college options. I hadn't decided yet on whether I would change my major. I really had to figure that out soon.

"I can do an hour at most. My boyfriend is home from the academy."

"Maiken is? I would like to meet him. Coach Dean talks about him all the time." His tone led me to believe he was truly serious and somewhat infatuated with my boyfriend. Or maybe he wanted to meet Maiken to see why Coach Dean put him up on a pedestal.

"Why?" I asked as we walked into the barn.

But my question flew out of my brain when my gaze landed on the floor.

I gasped.

Trevor took off in an all-out sprint, dropping to his knees to help Daddy, who was laid out like he was dead.

No. No. No.

A silent scream left my mouth as the barn began to spin. I shook my head hard and blinked several times, hoping I was having a nightmare.

Trevor felt along Daddy's neck. "Quinn!" His deep voice snapped me out of my trance. "Call 911."

I fumbled in my pockets for my phone. *No!* I left it in my room. I rushed over to Trevor, feeling light-headed. "I need your phone."

He whipped it out, held it up to his face to unlock it, and shoved it at me. "Hurry. He has a weak pulse."

My fingers shook as I punched in the number.

"Nine, one, one. What's your emergency?" the sweet lady asked.

"M-my d-dad n-needs help." *Not a time to be stuttering, Quinn Thompson.*

Trevor snatched the phone from me. "I have a man in his late forties who has a weak pulse and is passed out." Trevor lifted Daddy's eyelids. "Pupils somewhat dilated. Thompson farm. Yes, ma'am." He pocketed his phone.

I watched in horrid fascination at how well composed he was and how he knew what he was doing.

Trevor tapped my dad's face. "Mr. Thompson."

Tears flowed hot and fast down my cold cheeks.

"Get your mom," Trevor ordered as though he were in charge.

Hell, he was, because I couldn't even craft a damn sentence or thought. All I kept thinking was that Daddy wasn't going to make it.

Don't think like that.

Mom? Crap.

Trevor felt for a pulse. "Oh shit." He began CPR. Trevor was giving my dad CPR.

I slapped a hand over my mouth.

"Get your mom!" Trevor said again in a tone that could scare a rat.

I heard him, but I still couldn't move. This couldn't be happening.

Trevor blew into Daddy's mouth then did chest compressions, counting to himself to kick-start Daddy's heart.

That thought snapped me out of my haze. My body thawed, and my feet began to move. I spun on my heel and raced up to the house faster than sprinters on an Olympic track, crying and praying Daddy didn't die.

Chapter 22

Maiken

I texted Quinn.

Me: *Hey, babe. Hope you're having a good day so far. I can't wait to see you. I'm stopping by school around lunch to say hi and talk to Coach Dean. What time is your lunch period?*

I set my phone down on the bathroom counter and was about to take a shower when my phone rang. Maybe Quinn was in between classes.

Liam's name lit up my screen.

I tapped Answer and immediately asked, "Dude, are you coming home for Thanksgiving?" With the NCAA in preseason, I didn't think Liam would make it home.

"I need your help," he rushed out. "Can you and your brothers head to the farm and feed the horses?" He sounded frantic. "I'm trying to get a flight now. If I can, I should be there early tonight. Carter is on his way from Boston. He'll be there before me. Please, dude. You got to go."

I rubbed a hand down my chest. "Slow down. What's going on?"

He sucked in a breath. "My dad had a heart attack." His voice hitched on the last two words.

My eyes flew wide open as I gawked at myself in the mirror. "Is he…" I couldn't bring myself to say the word. I clutched my chest, remembering when the military had shown up at the door to break the bad news to us about Dad. I pressed my fingers over my heart. It felt as though I had a Mack truck sitting on me.

I blew out breath after breath. Quinn must be going crazy. I started the shower to get my ass in gear. I had to take care of my girl.

"He's in surgery," Liam said. "Mom said something about a blockage, and if Trevor wasn't there, my dad wouldn't be alive."

"Trevor?" Surely he couldn't be talking about the same boy who was related to Sloane. What would he be doing on the Thompson farm?

"Some guy on the basketball team my dad just hired. Look, Quinn is a mess. When you're finished at the farm, make sure you get over to the hospital. She's going to need you."

He didn't have to tell me twice. "I'll wrangle some guys and take care of the horses. I'll have my mom head to the hospital to see if she can help in any way. Maybe the farm store?"

"Nah. My mom hadn't opened the store. All this happened about four thirty this morning in the horse barn. Quinn and Trevor found him. I gotta go. I'm at the airport. I'll see you soon, and thanks, man." He hung up.

I stood idle for a minute, my brain scrambling to figure out who else I could get in addition to my brothers. I knew just the person to call.

On the first ring, Coach Dean answered. "Maiken?"

"Coach, Mr. Thompson had a heart attack this morning. I need some guys to help me feed the horses." I imagined we might have to clean out the stalls too.

"Dear God," he mumbled. "Fill me in."

I gave him the rundown as I knew it from Liam. When I was done, I told my mom what had happened, rounded up my brothers, and we piled into the Suburban and headed to the farm.

Coach Dean was meeting us there with guys from the basketball team. We had more than enough hands to bang out the chores and ensure the animals were taken care of.

Four hours later, after back-breaking work, a hot shower, and a quick burger, I was rushing into the hospital. Coach Dean had spoken to Mrs. Thompson while we'd been at the farm, and he'd learned that her husband had to have open-heart surgery. She hadn't known much more at that point.

I hurried past people walking by and down to the bank of elevators. Mrs. Thompson had told Coach she was in a waiting room on the fourth floor.

I stabbed the button for the elevator and checked my phone. There was still no response from Quinn. I was going nuts with worry, and I was jonesing to get my arms around my girl.

When the elevator doors opened, I practically flung myself into it. I bounced on my feet as the car traveled slowly up one floor then two. When the bell finally dinged, I was ready to pry the doors open with my bare hands. Suffocation took on a whole new meaning as I waited for the door to open. When it finally did, I tore out of the car, searching in one direction then another for any sign of the lounge or waiting room.

A short lady in scrubs hurried by.

"Waiting room?" I asked.

She pointed ahead of her. "Around the corner on the right."

My feet clobbered on the floor, sounding like Apple's hooves on concrete, as I flew in that direction and into a stuffy, filled room. The tension was thick, and the sadness was so soupy, I again felt like I couldn't breathe.

Visions of my own dad danced before me. But when I laid eyes on the girl with butterscotch hair, I faltered to an abrupt stop.

Some big blond dude, who looked more like a wrestler, had his arm around Quinn, consoling her as she snuggled against his chest. What had my insides in a huge knot was the way he was rubbing her arm and resting his chin on her head like he was the love of her life.

Breathe, man. This isn't the time to show your jealousy. This definitely isn't the time to lift the dude and throw him out of the room, not with Mrs. Thompson crying next to Coach Dean.

When Quinn's mom cleared the tears from her eyes, she jumped up and smothered me in her arms. "Thank you. You're such a good boy." Her heartbeat was off the charts. "Liam told me you took care of the animals." She eased away, regarding me with puffy, red eyes and splotchy, ashen skin.

"Maiken?" Quinn's voice was raw and cracked. The pain in her voice felt like daggers in my chest. She dashed away tears from her swollen eyes as she stood next to her mom on shaky legs.

I hugged her to me, wanting desperately to take away her pain. I smoothed a hand down her mud-coated hair. It was a knot of tangles, and the funk of the farm burned my nose.

Smell or not, I didn't care. "I'm so sorry, baby." My own tears sprang free.

She bawled and shook as she held me as tightly as I was holding her.

Coach Dean gave me a weak grin as he consoled Mrs. Thompson, while Trevor sat like the Lone Ranger. His expression was a mix of pain and sadness.

I continued to soothe my girl as her cries became muffled. I wasn't leaving this spot for anything. I wasn't leaving her until I knew she was okay. She was mine to console, protect, cherish, and love. My heart was hers to keep forever.

She lifted up her head, blinking long, wet lashes. Her amber gaze was crestfallen, yet it contained so much love. "I can't lose my dad."

The word *dad* sent me back to the day Mom had broken down in a heap of tears. "I know, babe. I know. I love you," I whispered. Emotions clogged my throat as I dashed tears from her beautiful face.

I knew he had to have emergency open-heart surgery, but I wasn't quite sure what the prognosis was at that point, and I was afraid to ask, afraid I would set in motion another round of tears from both Quinn and her mom. Regardless, I didn't think I could speak anyway.

Mom always said, "Sometimes no words are needed. You have to just listen and be there for a person."

I helped Quinn to a chair next to her mom. I needed to sit, or else my legs would give out. Quinn's pain was my pain. Quinn's sorrow was mine too. Everything she was feeling, I could feel as strongly as her. Dad's death was front and center, and the memories of that awful day were suddenly wreaking havoc on my psyche.

Trevor slid over to the chair next to mine. "Hey, man. I'm Trevor."

"Maiken. Thanks for taking care of Quinn."

"Anytime," he said. "She's a great girl." He was smitten with Quinn. I could hear it in his voice and see it written all over his face.

She's all mine. So don't get any ideas. "The best."

Silence filled the ten-by-ten room, which had stark white walls, two posters of medical information, and a TV hanging from the ceiling in the corner, which was as dead as the eerie quietness.

"The doctor should be in anytime," Mrs. Thompson said. "What's taking so long? Surgery should've been done by now."

I wasn't knowledgeable on how long open-heart surgery took, but it had to be hours.

Just then, a short man in scrubs came in, taking off his cap. His expression was blank.

Mrs. Thompson and Quinn jumped up at the same time.

"Dr. Fleming," Mrs. Thompson rushed out. "Is my husband okay?"

Quinn held her mom's hand. Both of them were tense and breathing heavily.

I said a silent prayer.

"Your husband is out of surgery. Initially when we spoke, I thought he had two blocked arteries, but we found a third. We had to do a triple bypass. He's in ICU. He should be awake shortly."

"So he's going to be okay?" Quinn's voice cracked.

Dr. Fleming gave her a warm smile. "We'll see how he does within the next twenty-four hours."

Of course doctors couldn't or wouldn't say for sure if a patient would be okay.

"When can we see him?" Mrs. Thompson asked.

"I'll have a nurse come to get you in about an hour. Your husband was very lucky to have someone who knew CPR."

Quinn looked over her shoulder at Trevor and smiled through an ocean of tears. "Trevor saved him."

Dr. Fleming nodded his head of dark hair at Trevor. "Well done, son." Then he left.

Quinn returned but not to sit next to me. She commandeered the chair on the other side of Trevor and grabbed his hand. "I owe you so much."

He draped his arm around her. "I'm glad I was there."

My stomach felt like it dropped off a cliff. I didn't know if the jealousy coursing through me was blinding me or if what I was truly witnessing was real. But I got the crazy impression that Quinn was falling for the dude.

Chapter 23

Quinn

Darkness spilled in through the window in Daddy's hospital room. He'd been in and out of consciousness with the pain meds he was on. Carter was sitting on the floor with his legs kicked out and his head resting against the wall. Momma was sitting in a chair butted up to Daddy's bed. Liam hadn't arrived yet. His flight was delayed.

I'd chewed every one of my nails off since Daddy had been rushed to the hospital, and I'd shed enough tears to last a lifetime. My stomach had a boulder in it, and I still smelled like the pigpen. But I didn't care. I wasn't leaving until I could talk to Daddy and see him at least smile.

I didn't know what we were going to do with the farm.

As if Carter were in my head, he said, "I'm going to head home and feed the animals."

We had no one to help us except Trevor. I had yet to ask him how he knew CPR, but it didn't really matter. I was just thankful he'd been there. I'd been a deer in the headlights, and if it weren't for him, Daddy would be dead.

I popped up off the chair on the other side of Daddy's bed. "Do you want me to go with?" I wanted to stay, but the farm was too much work for one person.

Carter held up a hand. "Stay with Mom. I can handle it."

"Call Maiken and Trevor. I'll give you their numbers. They can help." Maiken had been a godsend in taking care of the horses that morning. I wasn't sure if Trevor knew what to do since he'd barely started working at the farm.

"Son," Momma said, sounding like she was losing her voice. "Please put a sign up on the farm store window, letting our customers know we'll be closed for a few days."

Carter kissed Momma on the head. "I will. I got this, Mom. Just take care of Dad." Carter headed for the door.

I sent a quick text to Carter with Maiken and Trevor's numbers as I walked out with him. "What are we going to do? Daddy won't be able to do anything for a long time."

The doctor had informed Momma that it would be a good six months before Daddy fully recovered, barring any complications. I couldn't handle the farm by myself. I would certainly try, but Carter just might get his wish and have to take a break from college.

He gave me a glum grin. "I'm not returning to college anytime soon. No worries."

"I'm sorry, Carter."

He hugged me. "Don't be. It's not the reason I wanted to ditch college, but you know how I felt about it. Let me get home. I'll be back as soon as I can. I'll check where Liam is too." He started to leave.

"Carter, we need to make sure Liam doesn't drop out." Liam had a scholarship and was just starting basketball season. We had to support him while Carter and I picked up the slack.

"I know. We'll talk." Then he ambled down toward the elevators as though he didn't want to leave either.

Combing my hand through my knotted and dirty hair, I inched back into the room. I felt horrible that I wasn't going with Carter. But my brother and the farm instantly vanished from my thoughts when Daddy's eyes fluttered open.

Momma flew out of her chair. "Jeff."

I ran to the other side of his bed. "Daddy?" My pulse sped up. My heart was beating so fast I knew it would push out of my chest. "Daddy?"

Momma grasped his hand, and I took his other one.

"Water." His voice was low, cracked, and sounded as though he had been a smoker all his life.

Momma obliged.

I rubbed Daddy's arm. Too many emotions were hitting me at once. He was alive. He was breathing. He was so lucky.

I recited the Our Father prayer in my head as I gave him a warm, teary-eyed smile.

Momma set the cup down on the table beside his bed. "You gave us quite the scare." A river of tears spilled down her cheeks. "I'm so mad at you."

Momma had informed Carter and me earlier that she'd been pushing Daddy to make an appointment for a physical. He'd been light-headed recently, and she'd suspected it was his high blood pressure. He wasn't religious about taking his daily medication. However, it turned out his cholesterol was quite high, hence the blockages in his arteries.

His eyes fluttered shut briefly. "Hazel, darling. I love you, woman."

I couldn't hold back any longer. I cried and laughed while so many emotions clawed their way out.

Momma buried her face in the crook of Daddy's neck, sobbing.

"I promise I will listen to you from now on," Daddy said. Then he turned his head toward me. "Pumpkin, are the animals okay?"

I laughed harder as tears flowed freely. "Don't worry about the animals. Carter is home. He's taking care of them."

Relief washed over Daddy. The man was worried about his animals instead of himself. But that was Daddy. He'd grown up on a farm, and even though our animals put food on our table and paid the bills, he adored every cow, pig, horse, and chicken we had.

Regardless, I was ready to scream at him. But that wouldn't accomplish anything. He needed love and support.

Momma straightened and blew her nose into a tissue.

"I'm sorry, Daddy." A tiny part of me felt like I'd been the cause of his heart attack. He hadn't been the same since I'd gotten drunk. He'd been quieter and in some ways colder toward me. I knew I had to regain his trust. I knew he'd been disappointed at what I'd done. It also hadn't helped that someone had taken the pigs for the senior prank. I blamed myself for that too. If I hadn't had the party, then maybe some kid wouldn't have conjured a stupid idea of bringing pigs to school.

Momma's eyebrows drew down as Daddy squeezed my hand. "This isn't your fault."

"You've been upset since I threw that party," I said. "Stressed to the max."

"Quinn," Momma said.

I swished saliva around in my mouth. "I know." My shoulder twitched. "Daddy's health isn't great. But I can't help but feel guilty for what I did." I lifted Daddy's hand up to my mouth and pecked the back. "I can't lose you, Daddy."

I wasn't sure I could go to college. Granted, college was a long way off, and Daddy should be back to normal by then, but after heart surgery, he couldn't take care of the farm on his own. I would do whatever it took to make sure my dad stayed around to see me get married and have kids. He would be the best grandfather a kid could have.

Chapter 24

Maiken

Quinn lay in my arms, her head on my chest, one leg entwined with mine. "I don't want you to go."

I slipped my hand into the back pocket of her jeans, gazing up at the rafters in the barn that Ethan and I had turned into a makeshift gym. The space wasn't anything like Quinn's barns and certainly didn't have animal dung lingering in the air.

At the moment, I was inhaling Quinn's lavender shampoo. "I don't either. But I'll be home in a few weeks for Christmas break."

She shuddered. "Maiken, where do you think we'll be next year?"

Every muscle in me seized. "What kind of question is that?" Since I'd seen her in the hospital with Trevor, I couldn't shake the impression that she was into him. There was no question in my mind that he was infatuated with my girl. Anyone could see that by the way he'd been holding her—gentle, soft, and caring.

Like hell is he getting his paws on her. I knew Quinn loved me. I knew I could trust her. Trevor, on the other hand? No fucking way. Quinn was extremely vulnerable at the moment.

Her dad was still in the hospital and, barring any complications, would be home next week. Thank God he was doing well. According to the doctor, Mr. Thompson should make a full recovery, although he had a long road ahead.

Quinn traced lazy circles on my abdomen, her head resting under my chin. "I know you'll be a star basketball player at a big school, but I can't go to college. I have to be here for my dad." She snuggled deeper into me. "Anyway, do you think we'll be together?"

I couldn't imagine a life without Quinn. Sure, we were about to embark on an adult life of college and new experiences, but I didn't want to do any of that without her.

"I am yours, babe. My heart is yours to keep. So no matter the distance between us, I will be there for you." I thought we'd done a pretty good job at keeping our relationship strong while I'd been at the academy. "We've had great practice too. We're doing great." At least I thought we were. The separation was tough, and it probably wouldn't get any easier, but Mom and Dad had made their relationship work with him always on a military mission.

I remembered something Dad had said a time or two. *"Being away from your mother and you kids only makes my love stronger. I'm working for you guys and a better life."*

"College won't be any different," I added. "We just have to make a strong effort to see one another."

"Liam and Celia broke up when he left for college. They both wanted to see other people." She sounded frightened.

I threaded my fingers in her hair. "Do you want to play the field?" *If she says yes, I will fucking die.*

She lifted her head, digging her chin into my chest and batting her big amber eyes at me. "Hell no. I want to make sure you don't either."

I grabbed her waist. "Come here."

She crawled up until her body was flush with mine.

"The only field I want to play is one with you in it. I'm serious, Quinn. You're it for me. I couldn't imagine anyone else making me laugh and cry, or holding my hand, my heart, and my soul. I would die if I didn't get to kiss you ever again."

She blinked away a tear before crashing her mouth to mine, showing me her answer. Her tongue slipped in, tangling with mine.

Nothing else mattered in that moment but her and me and the way she made me feel—whole, happy, elated, and feeling as if I were on top of the world.

My hands roamed up and down her body, making her moan. Our kiss became wild, frantic, and passionate to the point that my body was on fire.

She nibbled on my lip, slowing the kiss. "Remember that surprise I mentioned to you on the phone a couple of weeks ago?" She swallowed, her cheeks turning red. "I'm on the pill."

Whoa! I wasn't expecting that, but my body reacted instantly—tingling, hard, and throbbing in one specific place.

She giggled, pressing her hips into mine. "I'm ready. You are too."

No doubt. Still, my stomach was in knots as I took in a deep breath.

She looked around. "We're alone." She lifted her eyebrows, sinking her teeth into her bottom lip. "I think we should. Now is a perfect time." She pressed her hands to my chest, sitting up and straddling me.

We were in a dark corner of the barn, a small carved-out space where Ethan and I had set up a lounge of sorts with blankets and even an old chair Mom didn't want in the house anymore.

I was ready, yet I wasn't. Although was there ever a right time? If two people loved each other and both were in agreement, then sex was a natural next step.

"Your family is out shopping," she said.

The coast was clear. And we certainly didn't have the threat of her dad finding us.

She began to unbuckle my belt, watching me watch her.

Once we lost our virginity, things would change between us. It could make our relationship stronger. Or she could find out I wasn't any good in the sex department and dump me.

Shut up, I shouted at the voice in my head.

"Maiken." Quinn's silky voice made me blink. "We both want this. Right?"

I lifted up to rest on my elbows, studying my gorgeous girlfriend, who suddenly had a sour expression. "More than anything. Fuck, I've been ready for like ever."

She giggled. "Well, I want you."

"Do you think it will change anything between us?"

She was still holding her bottom lip hostage. "If anything, it will bring us closer." She began to remove her sweater, showing milky-white skin.

Suddenly, my brain shut down, and my body took over like I didn't have any control over myself.

In a matter of minutes or maybe seconds, my gorgeous girl was in nothing but her lacy bra and panties, sitting on me, and looking like a goddess with her hair spilling down around her.

Holy hell!.

My mouth went bone dry. My body heated, and my hands had a mind of their own, rubbing a path up her abs and slowly creeping higher.

Her breathing became shallow, as did mine.

We locked eyes, a deeper connection gluing us together, one that said she was my everything and I was hers. Nothing in the world could break the bond we had.

I swore the door to my heart opened wider. I hadn't thought I could love her any more than I already did, but in that moment, she was the most beautiful angel in my world.

I pulled her down so our bodies were flush. Our lips joined, and the nerves coursing through me quieted as we got lost in us.

Chapter 25

Quinn

Snow fell as I sat on the front porch step waiting for Celia to pick me up. She was late, and if she didn't get there in the next five minutes, we were going to be late for our first class.

I was about to call her when my phone rang. Maiken's handsome face brightened my screen. I hit the answer button, and FaceTime connected.

He was standing in his dorm room with no shirt on. Our unexpected intimate rendezvous the previous day flashed before me. Actually, I couldn't sleep last night, and I hadn't been able to eat since either. Losing my virginity was tense yet freeing. Maiken had been gentle, soft, and just as nervous as I'd been.

He grinned, his blue eyes gleaming. "Are you okay?" He'd asked me the same thing several times as we'd lain on the floor of his barn afterward.

Momma had been right. The first time had hurt, but not as bad as I thought it would. Still, I had a deeper connection with him, a love so potent that I was ready to burst.

I giggled. "More than okay. You?"

"I feel…" He ran a hand through his wild hair. He looked as though he'd just gotten out of bed. "Like I'm walking on water. I want to see you, like, right now."

A cozy shiver blanketed me. "If I had a car, I would ditch school today and drive up to the academy."

"So no regrets?" He lost his smile, and trepidation took its place.

I shook my head. "Absolutely not. You?" I held my breath.

He leaned into the camera. "I want to do it a thousand more times with you."

Butterflies went wild in my stomach, and heat covered my body like a warm blanket on a snowy day. "Me too."

He chuckled. "I got to get ready for school. I love you, babe."

Headlights bounced down the driveway as Celia pulled in.

"Celia's here. Love you to the stars and back." I blew him a kiss. "Talk later." I ended the call before I jumped through the phone or decided to bribe Celia to drive up to the academy.

I darted down the porch steps, when Momma came out of the house. "Quinn, please make sure you're home right after school. You're working at the farm store today."

"I know, Momma. Love you. Kiss Daddy for me." I jogged the short distance to the car.

"You guys be careful," Momma called out. "The news just reported that roads are slick with black ice."

I hopped in. "Black ice?"

"That's why I'm late," Celia said. "I was driving like a grandma." The wipers cleared the droplets of snow from the windshield as Celia backed out.

I adjusted the heater in my direction. "Maiken and I did it yesterday."

Her neck snapped in my direction. "Oh, hell no. You can't tell me this while I'm driving."

I pointed at the road. "Pay attention. Black ice, remember."

She huffed as she traveled super slow down the two-lane country road. "Tell me everything." She sounded more excited than I did at the moment.

We'd promised each other we would tell the other when we stepped into womanhood. She hadn't yet. She and Liam had never taken that step.

I let out a contented sigh. "It was tense and beautiful and unexpect-ed." The boy I fell in love with, who had the bluest eyes on the planet, made my heart sing even more than ever before. I felt as though we had sealed our relationship forever.

She adjusted the hat on her head, glancing at me. "You do look different."

I rolled my eyes. "Please." I pulled down the visor to check myself in the tiny mirror just the same. "I don't see anything different. You're full of it."

She snorted then laughed. "We're growing up, Quinn. I'm not sure if I'm happy about that or not."

I closed the visor. "I know what you mean." I thought of Daddy and the farm. I was seriously considering not applying to any college. "I think I might take a year off after high school."

Again, her gaze rounded to me. "What?"

I stabbed a finger at the windshield. "Road, please."

"You're going to give up your dream of being a doctor?"

"I might change my major to teaching actually." I hadn't had a chance to share that with her yet.

She pumped the brakes, slowing to a stop way before the stop sign. "You would make a great teacher."

"Thank you, bestie. But with Daddy's health, I have to stay and help. I can take classes at the community college at night."

"What about your brothers? Surely Liam isn't going to drop out. Please tell me he isn't. He's got a great gig with his scholarship, a once-in-a-lifetime gig for that matter."

"He's not," I said. "He wanted to, but Carter and I convinced him not to. Besides, Trevor, Noah, and Dustin are helping for the short term, especially since we're selling Christmas trees now."

With the coast clear of any cars, Celia turned right. "I can help too. My mom only needs me in the wee hours of the morning. I'll help at the farm store after school."

It was humbling that friends were rallying to help us. Momma was going to talk to a couple of Daddy's friends from church too. She wanted to find someone who could be on the farm during the day, helping Carter, since Trevor, Noah, and Dustin had school. Coach Dean had offered to help as well.

The snow continued to fall as we slowly made our way to school.

"Okay," Celia said. "Since we're on the topic of growing up and college and stuff, what about the prom? Are you going to go? I found out from Elise, who's on the prom committee, that the theme is the Roaring Twenties."

"I hadn't thought about the prom." Given my luck with parties and dances, I wasn't sure I wanted to attend. However, it was my senior year.

"Maiken will have a prom to go to at the academy. So you'll have two."

"You know parties, dances, and proms are bad for me and Maiken."

She tittered. "What could go wrong? Come on. It's our last hoorah in high school. We've got to go. And it will be cool to pick out an outfit for the Roaring Twenties."

"Let's get through the next couple of months." I wanted to wait to plan things after my dad came home.

The roads were much clearer in town as Celia zipped through the side streets of Ashford. "Fair enough. Now, one more thing. I heard from Elise that Trevor's girlfriend, Claire, has it out for you."

My neck swiveled in her direction so fast I got whiplash. "Come again? That's nonsense."

"Sure, but put yourself in her shoes. You have been spending a lot of time with Trevor since you're tutoring him, and then he gets a job on your farm. How would you feel?"

Oh my God. I wondered if Maiken thought the same thing. When he'd walked into the hospital, I'd been snuggled up to Trevor, crying. I'd also been bragging about how Trevor was a hero.

"What's wrong? It looks like you've seen a ghost. Please tell me you and Trevor—"

"Hell no," I said in a rush as my blood coagulated. "Maiken probably thinks the same." I definitely had to talk to Maiken, although he'd given me no indication he was jealous.

Why would he be? Your dad just had a heart attack. You were distraught, and Maiken wasn't the type to lash out in dire situations.

"After your tryst with Maiken yesterday, I doubt he thinks anything of the sort."

She had a point. Maiken had shown me nothing but love, love, and more love. And if I knew Maiken, he would've broached the subject of Trevor and how he didn't like him touching me or around me if it bothered him. I'd seen firsthand how he had dealt with Chase Stevens when Chase was interested in me. Not only that, he'd been cordial to Trevor when he'd met him. I decided not to bother Maiken about Trevor. He and I were in a great place, and I wanted to keep that momentum going.

The school loomed in the distance.

"Well, be on the lookout in case Claire confronts you."

I shrugged. "She can, but I'm not interested in Trevor."

I didn't need any more drama in my life. I knew that was a tall order since high school wasn't over with yet.

Chapter 26

Quinn

I sighed as I walked into the gym. Life wasn't spinning out of control as it had been since the start of summer. Christmas came and went in a blur, as did school leading up to the holidays.

Daddy was on the mend, thank the Lord. Each day that passed, he got better and better. However, his mood was a different story. He barely smiled, and he seemed depressed. He tried to help Carter and me, but Momma threatened to tie him up if he so much as lifted a finger to do anything around the farm. Carter and I did the same— Carter more so than me. My brother was a lot like Daddy, not taking crap from anyone.

The farm was in good hands with my brother. He was staunch in his drive to make sure the farm was a well-oiled machine. He and I settled into a routine, much like Daddy and I had before his heart attack. We also had plenty of help. Trevor was in a groove and fitting in well with Carter, plus he was a hard worker. Apparently, he needed the money. He didn't go into detail as to why, even though I'd tried to probe a little.

Trevor's business wasn't mine, and I had my own things to do. Noah and Dustin were also pitching in when they could, and Coach Dean had the basketball team working at the farm one morning a week.

"It's good for your soul," Coach Dean had told them one morning before they'd gotten started. "Plus, it builds character and teaches you what it means to work together as a team."

I would never forget when Maiken had played for Coach, and the team had gotten up at the crack of dawn to clean out the horse stalls. Maiken hadn't complained, but Chase Stevens sure had.

Regardless, it was nice to have help. I didn't have to bust my butt as hard, so I could dedicate more time to my schoolwork or to making sure Daddy didn't try to strap on his boots and gloves to lend a hand.

Shoes squeaked along the hardwood as Noah, Trevor, and the team played a practice game. Coach Dean was watching them intently with a scowl. He hadn't been thrilled with their performance so far that season. They had played half of their scheduled games, and the team's stats were five wins and eight losses.

On the other hand, Maiken was having a great season. He'd been instrumental in helping the team win thirteen games with only one loss.

Coach Dean blew his whistle. "Take five. Then we'll finish up with some defensive plays."

The team scattered to grab water and towels.

The cheerleaders were huddled on the far end, and Tessa was speaking animatedly with her hands. All the girls were listening to her intently except for Claire. Trevor's girl zeroed in on me then on Trevor. I was surprised she hadn't lashed out at me since Celia had warned me weeks ago.

Trevor had suggested that we use my kitchen as a place for tutoring, which made sense. He and I worked, and then I tutored him. Sometimes Momma would invite Trevor to stay for dinner. Daddy often insisted he did. Trevor and Daddy had bonded, and Daddy couldn't stop thanking him for saving his life.

I started to climb the bleachers to join my BFF, when Coach Dean called my name. "Quinn, a moment." He ambled across the court, swiping a hand over his bald head. "I just want to say thank you for helping Trevor. He's all caught up on his classes, and his grades are good."

"My pleasure. He's a nice guy and seems to want to do well." I hadn't gotten that creepy vibe since the first day I'd met Trevor. In my opinion, he was looking for attention. I knew little of his home life except that he and his dad lived with Sloane and her mom.

Whatever Sloane had been warning me about when it came to Trevor hadn't been there. If he and Sloane didn't get along, I wouldn't know. Trevor never mentioned Sloane or talked about her or his family with me.

"He's had a tough road," Coach said in a low voice.

I raised an eyebrow. "Is he okay?"

He briefly glanced over his shoulder. "I think working on the farm has steered him in the right direction."

"Well, Daddy adores him."

"I hear. Your father respects Trevor. So, Liam made it back to school?"

"He did." Liam had wanted to stay home and help, but the family wouldn't let him, although we'd had to get Coach Dean to talk to him to convince him to go back to school.

"Good. That boy is going places. Anyway, let your dad know I'll be by later." He blew his whistle as he returned to the team.

Trevor grinned at me, drinking from a water bottle.

I smiled then climbed up to sit next to Celia.

"Claire is glaring at you," Celia said.

I set my backpack down on the bench beside me. "I don't know why she's jealous. It's not like Trevor and I are chummy chummy."

"Seriously." She closed her laptop. "Anyone can see he likes you."

"Okay. But I don't like him as boyfriend material. And I don't hang out with him."

"But he does work on your farm, girl."

"Let's talk about something else, like college. Any offer letters come in yet?"

Celia and I had filled out applications right after Thanksgiving. The deadline had been January first with a decision expected no later than April first. Since we were only in late January, I didn't expect to hear anything, but Celia had submitted her applications a week before me.

"Nothing yet from Emerson College or BU." As a communications major, those were her top two choices.

"Me either. I just talked to Mrs. Flowers. She said BU and Boston College usually send out letters between mid-February to mid-March." I'd decided to switch my major to teaching and had applied to both of those schools. I had many other options for great colleges and universities around the country, but I wanted to stay local. In case my parents needed me, I would be close by.

"What about Maiken?" she asked.

Shrugging, I watched the players set up under the basket while Coach Dean explained a defensive play. "A scout from Boston College is interested in him. I'm not sure where that stands since he froze on court that day we were at the game." Daddy's heart attack had taken up much of my brain space, so thoughts of college weren't high on my list. Not to mention, whenever we had a chance to see each other, nothing but him and me mattered. "I still can't believe we're so close to graduation and how our lives have changed."

"You mean sex," she whispered, waggling her eyebrows.

"Well, that's for sure. Maiken and I can't get enough of each other when he's home. But it's not just that. We're getting older. Our lives are about to change. It's kind of scary to step into the unknown— meeting new people, experiencing new things, building a future."

"It sounds like you're writing your valedictorian speech."

"I've been working on it." My grades had gotten so much better, thanks in part to sleeping more, working less, and tutoring Trevor. While he'd been doing his exercises or reading, I'd had a chance to do my own homework. "How's your project coming for the school's blog?"

She'd been busy covering the sports games and seemed to be in her element. Not only was she good at writing for the school blog and covering high school sports, but she really seemed to love it. She was a natural in front of the camera too.

"I'm almost done. I've interviewed each basketball player. When you came in, I was working on Trevor's story."

I raised an eyebrow. "Coach just told me he's had a tough road. Has he mentioned anything to you?"

We both watched the team run through plays.

She chewed on her bottom lip. "His mom passed away last year from a heart attack."

I gaped. "For real?" Now it made sense how he'd jumped into action when we found Daddy on the floor of the barn.

"Yeah. I asked him how he knew CPR. He told me he learned not long after he'd lost his mom."

I eyed Trevor, who was going in for a layup. "I didn't know."

"He said he doesn't like to talk about it. He does want to be a paramedic if basketball doesn't pan out for him. Anyway, students will read all about the Kensington basketball players when the story goes live on the blog next week."

"I'm still curious why Sloane hates Trevor. He's a nice guy."

"Maybe because he's disrupted her life. Him and his dad anyway. Sloane and her mom were moving. Then they weren't, and all of a sudden, she has a stepbrother. I can get behind that. I wouldn't be happy to have complete strangers living in my house." Celia nudged me. "Here comes trouble."

"Double trouble," I mumbled.

Claire and Tessa glided over like they were above anyone else. That was Tessa's MO. I didn't know much about Claire except for the snarls and glares she shot my way anytime we would run into each other in the hall or cafeteria.

Tessa tossed her inky-black hair over her shoulder. "Quinn, please tell me Dustin doesn't have to work on the farm anymore."

I deadpanned. "I don't have any say in what he does."

Claire cocked her hip. "You should tell Trevor too."

I checked on Trevor to see if he'd heard her, but he was running toward the basket at the other end of the court.

"You two sound jealous," Celia said. "Maybe you both should consider working on the farm. You know, with the pigs."

Tessa feigned a laugh as her pink-painted lips twisted. "For all we know, Celia, you were responsible for the running of the pigs that first day of school."

We still didn't know who the culprit was, and frankly, that whole incident was in the past. With Daddy's health, we'd all but forgotten about it. Daddy didn't need the stress anyway.

"Yeah, like, why would I do that?" Celia asked. "You're the one capable, Tessa. You would do anything to cause trouble for Quinn."

Claire twirled strands of her brown hair around her finger and glanced over her shoulder at Trevor, I suspected. "Whoever it was had to be strong and have the means to transport pigs."

Celia and I exchanged a perplexing look.

"Do you know who that person is, Claire?" I got the impression she did.

Surely Trevor hadn't pulled the prank, or maybe that was the reason Sloane had warned me about him. Still, Trevor wasn't the only strong boy in school. Noah came to mind as I watched him go in for a layup. He had the muscles too.

Claire's brow lifted. "Of course not. I've never been on your farm or any farm."

Trevor had, though, the night of my party.

Tessa lowered her gaze to her white Nikes as though she knew something. Maybe Celia was right. Maybe Tessa had a hand in the prank or knew the guilty party.

"Tessa, do you know something about the pigs?" I asked. Not that I could do anything to that person other than give him or her a piece of my mind. I didn't want to rehash the ordeal since it would raise Daddy's blood pressure.

"You're smoking dope," Tessa exclaimed. "You know I hate pigs."

"You do know something," Celia chimed in, studying her.

Tessa's mouth dropped, and she shook her head. "Why would you think that?" Her voice had an edge to it, not bitchy, but scared.

I was ready to fly down the bleachers and pummel her. "Unbelievable. You know, I can hear it in your tone. Who was it?"

She huffed. "There's nothing you can do now."

Motherpucker.

"Who?" My tone echoed around the gym.

The team stopped playing, and Coach Dean glanced at us.

I ran down the bleachers. "Who, Tessa? Who brought the pigs to school?"

Claire slid to Tessa's side as though she could protect her friend.

Noah rushed over along with Trevor. Even Coach Dean came closer.

I stuck my hands on my hips so I wouldn't punch her.

Tears pooled in her eyes. "It was my idea." She looked at Noah.

He raised his hands. "I didn't want to do it."

My head spun. Noah was one of the good guys, or so I'd thought. "You've got to be kidding. Does Maiken know?"

Coach Dean's features hardened. "Team, practice is over. Noah, Tessa, I want you two to have a seat."

Claire threw herself at a tired-looking Trevor. He caught her as he gave me a sad smile.

The team didn't want to leave. Drama was about to unfold, and high schoolers salivated for drama.

Coach pointed at the exit. "Hit the showers, or else all of you will be doing fifty laps around the track tomorrow."

Trevor, along with the rest of the team, obeyed, and Claire followed her boyfriend out.

Noah planted his butt on the bottom bleacher, fear swimming in his gray eyes.

Tessa huffed as she sat next to him, pouting.

I crossed my arms over my chest, wanting nothing more than to scream at them. They had no idea what they'd put my dad through. He'd had to pay to have cameras installed, which weren't cheap. He'd worried constantly about someone pulling another prank using our animals. Not only that, the stress hadn't helped his health.

Coach Dean settled in front of them. "Talk."

"I told them not to do it," Noah said. "But Dustin wouldn't listen."

"Shut up," Tessa said to Noah.

"Dustin?" Shock rode my tone. I hadn't seen that one coming.

Come to think of it, he had been close by when the pigs ran down the hall. Tessa had too. And Noah had been late that day.

"It was Tessa's idea," Noah said.

Coach Dean pinched his chin with his fingers. "Here's what's going to happen. Noah, you're benched for three games. I should bench you for the rest of the season, but I'm not going to. Principal Sanders will have a say in the rest of your penance. Ms. Stevens, since you were the mastermind behind the prank, I'm going to recommend you be suspended for a week."

Tessa straightened, fear washing over her. "You can't do that. I've got exams, and this won't look good for me."

"You should've thought about that before you took my pigs," I said.

"I'll speak to Dustin," Coach said. "He'll have to answer to the principal as well. Now I can't order you, Ms. Stevens, to apologize to the Thompson family, but I can order you, Noah. If you want to play for me next year and for the rest of this season, you'll get over to the Thompson farm and speak to Quinn's parents. Is that clear?"

"Yes, sir," he said to Coach while giving me puppy-dog eyes.

"Is that why you and Dustin were quick to help out at the farm?" I asked. Carter had told me Dustin and Noah didn't want to get paid. Noah had pulled extra shifts outside of the one he'd done with the basketball team.

He nodded.

Coach wagged his finger at Noah then Tessa. "I'll see both of you in the principal's office in the morning." He harrumphed as he shook his head and left the gym.

Celia came down from the bleachers. "What a shocker. This is front-page news for sure. Tessa Stevens, the girl who hates pigs, the same girl who put on a show that morning, blaming Quinn for the prank."

Tessa popped up. "You are not going to put that in the school's blog."

"I most certainly am," Celia said, oozing confidence and excitement.

Tessa stomped her foot before she ran out.

Noah rose. "Quinn, I'm so, so sorry." He sounded sincere.

"Tell that to my dad," I said, spinning on my heel to leave.

I wasn't as mad as I'd been the day the prank happened. I was more annoyed. Even though it was water under the bridge, they did owe my parents an apology.

I was about ten feet from the door when Maiken walked in.

My jaw bounced on the floor as Tessa, Noah, Dustin, and pigs flew out of my mind.

What is Maiken doing here?

Maiken grinned at me, but it never reached his gorgeous blue eyes. "Surprise."

It took me a second to get my brain to fire. Then I was rushing up to him. "What happened?"

"I messed up my back."

I slapped a hand over my mouth. "How?" *Oh my God!* He'd been doing so well and had worked so hard to get back in tip-top shape for basketball.

"I got knocked down in the game a couple of nights ago. Mom made me an appointment with my doctor in Ashford. I need to get back to the academy tonight, though."

I threw my arms around him. "I'm so sorry. Did the doctor say what's wrong?"

His hands slid around my waist as he pecked me on my lips. "I'm waiting on him to call with the results of the MRI I had earlier. He suspects it's just muscle spasms. I think it is too, but I want to be sure it's not one of my discs. I can't be out. There's a scout from Gonzaga coming to my game next week, and the scout from Boston College is returning to watch me as well. Actually, he wants to chat with me."

My heart fluttered at the idea that he could get a scholarship to BC. That would mean he and I could be together, at least in the same city. BC and BU weren't that far apart. What didn't sit well with me was Gonzaga. That school was located on the opposite side of the country.

Chapter 27

Maiken

My pulse was all over the place as I walked into Coach Green's office. We'd just tacked another win under our belt, leaving us with only one loss the entire season. We had six games left to play, and we were primed to head to the state playoffs.

I'd missed three of our last five games because of my back. I'd been fortunate that I hadn't slipped a disc, but the muscle spasms had kept me from playing.

Mr. Patrick, the scout from BC was relaxed in a chair in front of Coach's desk while Coach said, "I have the fishing trip set up for July if you're interested."

Coach was a big fisherman and preferred ocean fishing mostly. When he retired, he wanted to move to a sleepy town on the Gulf Coast of Florida and do nothing but fish. His office was even drenched with pictures of big fish he'd caught.

Coach waved at the seat next to Mr. Patrick. "Sit, Maiken."

I shook Mr. Patrick's hand before I sat down. "Nice to meet you, sir."

I hadn't had a chance to meet the man before now. However, Coach had pointed him out in the stands before our game earlier.

Mr. Patrick rose, smoothing a hand over his red tie. "You were good out there tonight, Maiken."

My rapid pulse came down a notch. "Thank you, sir."

Once we were both seated, Mr. Patrick turned his body slightly toward me. "Where do you see yourself in five years?"

I had no idea how the conversation would go, but Coach had given me a heads-up that Mr. Patrick would ask about life beyond college.

I straightened my spine. "I would love to play for the NBA one day."

"What if you couldn't?" Mr. Patrick asked.

I'd pondered that very question a million times. "I've thought about the military and maybe one day coaching at the high school level." I flicked a quick look at Coach.

He had a proud expression.

"The college certainly offers several different majors, like teaching, if that's what you had in mind."

I hadn't considered teaching, but if I wanted to coach, a teaching degree would be a good first step. And how cool would that be for Quinn and me to teach at the same school?

I grinned at Mr. Patrick. "It might be." Dad had always said to make sure I planned for life after the NBA.

"There's no need for you to decide on a major right now. Maiken, the sports director, coach, and I are very pleased with what we've seen on your tapes. I'm extremely happy with what I saw out on that court tonight. Your skills have improved greatly since I watched you play back in October at the scrimmage game. And Coach Green here"—he tipped his head at his friend—"has done a great job molding you. Your three-point shots are effortless. It's evident you're a natural for the game."

"I can't take all the credit, Richard," Coach said as he leaned back in his chair. "Coach Dean at Kensington has done a fine job as well."

"My dad has too, sir. Well, before he passed away, that is."

A veil of sorrow flashed in Mr. Patrick's eyes. "He sure has, son. And an upstanding student too. Your grades show that. I only have one last question for you. On behalf of Boston College, we would like to extend an offer for you to play starting next year. But before you decide, we would also like to invite you to take a tour of the campus and check out the facilities."

I was ready to burst with glee and shout to the world that I'd done it. I had achieved something that I thought would never be possible given Dad's death, moving, my aunt dying of breast cancer, my family's struggles, and my accident. I didn't have to see the campus to give him my answer. While BC wasn't my first choice, there were so many good things about the school, the basketball program, the proximity to home, and to Quinn if she decided to attend a school in Boston. Mom would definitely be happy and proud.

I grinned from ear to ear. "I would love to visit the campus."

Mr. Patrick rose. "Glad to hear it. I'll be in touch with a date and time. I'll let Coach Green know as well. I need to get on the road."

"Before you head out," Coach Green said, "I need to talk to you about another matter. It will only take a minute."

That was my cue to leave, and I couldn't wait to run back to the dorm and tell Ethan and my other siblings. I also couldn't wait to call Mom and share the great news with Quinn, who was waiting for me in my dorm room.

After Mr. Patrick and I shook hands and I thanked him profusely, I hustled out of there. I jogged through the sports complex at breakneck speed. I felt as though a ten-ton weight had been lifted off my shoulders. I was about to play for a Division I school.

I burst through the doors and out into the cool night air. I ran all the way to my dorm then took the stairs two at a time, huffing and puffing.

When I burst into my dorm room, Quinn jumped up from her spot on my bed. Before she could say a word, I tackled her to the bed—gently, of course.

"BC wants me to play ball for them."

She squealed. "Oh my God! That's fantastic."

I was over the moon. I couldn't contain myself or control my hands or lips. I devoured all of her—her lips, her tongue, and everything I could get my hands and mouth on.

She giggled as we kissed like we hadn't seen each other in years. Ever since we'd started having sex, I couldn't get enough of her. Each time was better and better, and man, Kade had been so spot-on. Being in love with a person heightened the senses to the max. Quinn gave me a high like no other. When I was with her, I felt like I could fly. Our future was shaping up to be fantastic. I had my girl. I had an offer to play ball, and I would be close to my family. I couldn't ask for anything more.

I nibbled on her ear. "I love you, Quinn Thompson. You have made my life complete."

Her answer wasn't what I was expecting, but I wasn't complaining when she removed her top. "Noah and Ethan know to stay away."

Noah and Quinn had come up together for the game, which surprised me since she'd been mad at him for the part he'd played in the pig prank.

"He was sincere and very apologetic to Daddy," she'd told me. "And everyone deserves a second chance, even Tessa." According to Quinn, Tessa had even apologized to her parents.

I laughed. "You've been planning this?"

She pulled her bottom lip in between in her teeth. "Yep."

Man, she was gorgeous. Rosy cheeks, plump lips, and a body that was all mine. Hell, she was all mine, and one day she would be my wife.

But first we had to finish high school.

Chapter 28

Quinn

I couldn't believe we were in April, and our senior prom was next week. I debated whether I wanted to go. Maiken had bagged his prom at the academy. He wasn't interested in attending any proms.

"Homecoming was enough for me," he'd said.

I couldn't blame him. That had been the night Sloane had hit him with her car, the same night Marcus had too much to drink, and the same darn night that I'd almost knocked out Sloane's teeth.

I hadn't planned on going to my senior prom either. I had my valedictorian speech to finish. It wasn't anywhere near ready, and with exams coming up next month, I wanted to be ahead of the curve. The last I'd checked with Mrs. Flowers, I was still in the number-one spot, and barring any unforeseen hiccups, like failing a test, the prestigious award was mine to lose.

Still, Celia had convinced me to go to prom.

"Come on," she'd begged. "You'll regret not going. And I don't have a date."

Maybe I would look back and wonder why I didn't go. Besides, I couldn't let my best friend down.

I was almost at Celia's car when Trevor caught up to me. "Quinn."

I pivoted on my heel. "Hey, I'm in a hurry." Celia and I had shopping on our agenda for that afternoon.

He pushed his unruly blond hair out of his eyes and was about to say something when Claire ran up, sporting a sneer.

She dug her claws into Trevor's arm, a clear sign for me to back off. "You were supposed to meet me at your car." She pouted at Trevor.

He ignored her and asked me, "Is Maiken going to the prom with you?"

I studied him, wondering where he was going with his question.

Claire didn't wonder at all. "You are not taking her." Her tone was nasty and full of disgust.

I clenched my teeth. "I have a name."

She let go of Trevor. "You know, Quinn, I'm not holding back anymore. You are not so special." She waved her hand up and down my body. "You have no meat on your bones. Your breasts are flat. You look and smell like one of your pigs. And you dress like you just walked out of a thrift store."

I laughed, even though I was seething inside, even though my hands began to tremble around the straps of my backpack.

She bared her teeth. "Stay the fuck away from my boyfriend."

Trevor swung out his arm in front of Claire. "Seriously, Claire, how many times have I told you? Quinn and I are friends."

"You want to screw her." Claire's voice went up in pitch. "Maybe you already did." She skirted around Trevor and got in my face. "We only have a few weeks left of school, but I can make your life a living hell, which I should've done long before now."

And the claws finally come out.

I opened my arms. "Do whatever you want. I don't have time for your jealousy."

Between Claire's sneers and glares in the hall and Tessa giving me the middle finger anytime I saw her, I was done with the petty drama. Tessa deserved her one-week suspension. Noah deserved being benched by Coach Dean along with a one-day suspension, and Dustin had received a one-day suspension as well for the part he'd played.

Claire stuck out her chin. "Go near Trevor again, and you'll see what I'm made of."

Celia drove up and beeped the horn.

That was my cue to get out of Dodge. One thing I wouldn't miss about high school was the mean girls. I had no idea what college would be like, but I hoped I didn't have to deal with the Claires and Tessas of the world.

Trevor said something to Claire that I couldn't quite hear.

I ignored them and opened the passenger door of Celia's car.

"Quinn," Trevor said.

"Really?" Claire whined.

"Babe, back the fuck off. I am not asking Quinn to the prom."

She closed her mouth, pursing her red lips.

Trevor blew out a breath, seemingly frustrated. "I heard Maiken got into BC. Coach Dean told me Gonzaga made him an offer too. Which one did he decide on?"

"Let's go," Celia said. "We need to get there before the flapper dresses are picked through."

I quickly bent my head down. "One sec." Then I said to Trevor, "He accepted BC's offer last week." Maiken didn't want to move to Washington, and he wanted to play for a school that was part of the ACC conference.

"Cool. I've been considering BC when I graduate next year. Noah is even talking about playing for BC too. I'll catch Maiken when he comes home."

Claire glared daggers at me.

I was tempted to hug Trevor to say thank you for keeping Claire off me, but that would only give Claire more ammunition to make my life hell, and I didn't need the hassle. When it came to bullies, I'd been there, done that, and had gotten the T-shirt.

Instead, I slid into the passenger seat. "Oh, and Trevor, my mom's making your favorite for dinner tonight."

His green eyes lit up. "Roast beef? I'll be there."

Claire's nostrils flared, as she turned ten shades of red.

I shut the door. "Let's get out of here."

Celia sped out of the school lot. "What was all that about?"

"You were right. Claire wants my head on a platter."

"She better get hot, then. School is almost finished."

I shrugged. "Whatever. I think I'm immune to bullies anyway. I hope there aren't any at BC."

I'd gotten accepted to BU and BC, and I had decided on BC for two reasons. Maiken was going to BC, which was one big reason. And I also liked the atmosphere of the college. I hadn't received any scholarships, but I did qualify for financial aid, which was okay by me. My parents would help where they could, but I honestly didn't want to take a dime from them. It was time I did things on my own.

"I'm sure you'll have a Tessa or Claire at BC, but nothing like high school." Celia had gotten accepted to Emerson, which was eight miles from BC. So we would be close and could hang out and do things together.

I watched the houses in Ashford tick by. "I'm counting the days until graduation."

Celia slowed to a stop. "Forty-four days."

Forty-four days until Kensington High was in my rearview mirror. Forty-four days until I said goodbye to my high school years, which had been good, bad, and ugly.

Chapter 29

Quinn

Music pounded from the speakers as the band played "Rollercoaster" by the Jonas Brothers. I stood near the bar, people watching. It was fascinating to see kids let loose and grope and dance.

The Cave was the venue of choice for our senior prom, the same club managed by Kade Maxwell, Maiken's cousin. Kade didn't looked thrilled to be working that night. He'd been trying to keep law and order, but some of the kids were getting a bit rowdy near the bar.

I ignored them. I suspected they'd been drinking. I'd seen a few boys take out flasks from their suit jackets. Our prom wasn't the normal setup of previous proms. We didn't have a punch bowl on a table. We actually had bartenders behind the bar, serving soda, water, and virgin drinks like piña coladas and strawberry daiquiris. However, Kade had removed all the liquor bottles that were normally displayed on a shelf behind the bar.

I watched Celia make a fool of herself with Noah on the dance floor. Her sparkly white flapper dress swung along with her hips. Noah couldn't dance to save his life, but the two were having a good time.

The mood definitely gave me the sense that I was living in the Roaring Twenties, at least from some of the old movies I'd watched with my granny. Boys wore pinstripe suits. Like Celia and me, most girls wore flapper dresses, some long, some short. Their hairstyles fit the era along with their fancy hats and hair accessories.

My senior prom had officially begun. I couldn't believe I was even there, and without Maiken. I couldn't believe I was graduating in a few short weeks. My stomach churned with nerves and excitement. Memories of my high school days flashed before me as I held my virgin piña colada. I'd had some great times, but none greater than the day I met Maiken.

I collected the box and had just started to leave the storeroom when Celia flew in.

"O-M-G. You have got to see him." She practically dragged me out with her. I'd known Celia since the second grade, and I knew two things excited her—horses and Shawn Mendes. I didn't see a horse anywhere in the store, and there was no way Shawn Mendes would be in our small town in Massachusetts.

We settled in the doorway, looking out at the various customers milling around.

She leaned in. "He's over by the hats."

I followed her gaze, or more like her finger, which she had pointed at what Momma would call a tall drink of water.

"Isn't he dreamy?" Celia cooed.

The boy's sandy-blond hair was cut short on the sides like the men I'd seen in those military movies my dad loved to watch.

I wanted to ask her what had happened to her crush on Liam. Instead, I sighed like Celia had at the Shawn Mendes concert. The somewhat heavy box in my hand felt weightless.

Dreamy didn't begin to describe the boy at all. He had a strong jaw, a somewhat crooked nose as though he'd broken it in a fight, and a broad chest.

He tried on a beanie that my granny had made then examined himself in the small mirror we had on the counter for that very reason.

"I love how that Henley fits him," Celia said.

Dreamy Boy checked the price on the hat then returned it to the pile. My heart fell a notch. He was dressed nicely enough in jeans,

army boots, and no jacket, which seemed odd considering the tempera-
ture was around fifteen degrees outside.

"You should go talk to him," Celia said without looking at me.

I didn't know if he'd heard Celia or if he felt us staring, but he
lifted his head. When he did, I flinched and almost dropped the box.

Celia waved.

The blood drained from me. "Don't bring attention to us."

Granny had always said that one day, Celia would be trouble. I'd
laughed many times when I'd heard that. But I was beginning to think
that Granny had some foresight.

Regardless, I didn't need some boy to pick on me or look down at
me as if I were beneath him, and Dreamy Boy was giving me that vibe
until one side of his mouth turned up. Whether he was looking at Celia
or me, one thing was certain—my pulse galloped as fast as my horse,
Apple. I couldn't look away.

His big blue eyes sucked me in and gobbled me up. He had hair
like James Dean—thick, sandy blond, and longer on top. His pretty lips
were to die for. Yeah, I was crushing hard.

"A penny for your thoughts," a deep male voice said in my ear.

I blinked away that snowy November day to find Trevor staring
down at me. His blond hair was slicked back with gel, and his green
eyes seemed to glow in the dimly lit atmosphere. He looked dapper in
his bow tie and pinstripe suit complete with suspenders.

I scanned the immediate area for Claire. The girl would have a
hissy fit if she caught him talking to me. She'd already given me the
evil eye when I bumped into her earlier.

"Where's Claire?" I asked.

He tucked a hand in his slacks. "She went to the bathroom. She
might be there a while. The line is long."

I sighed. "I wish Maiken was here," I said more to myself.

I was happy Celia and I had come together, but as the song
morphed into a slow one, I wanted Maiken desperately. I wanted to
celebrate the end of our senior year together. I wanted to dance with
him. I wanted to hold him, kiss him, and feel his arms around me.

"I'm sorry," he said. "Care to dance?"

I painted on a fake smile. "Thank you, but I'll pass." Claire would have a cow if she saw Trevor and me dancing. But that wasn't the sole reason I said no. I just wasn't into dancing with anyone other than Maiken.

"So tell me, Quinn Thompson, who do you think will win king and queen tonight?"

He couldn't be serious. Who cared about that award? I didn't. I also knew I wouldn't be the queen of the ball.

Nevertheless, I giggled, losing some of my self-pity over Maiken not being there with me. "Tessa and Dustin."

Trevor bobbed his head in agreement. "You're probably right."

Dustin and Tessa were kissing on the dance floor. That could be Maiken and me.

Stop torturing yourself.

Noah had his arms around Celia, but both seemed stiff as they shuffled their feet next to Dustin and Tessa. We had extended the invitations to juniors after the school had canceled their prom due to low ticket sales.

Inwardly, I smiled. Celia liked Noah, but they weren't an item. I would bet she wasn't over Liam. They both had wanted to see other people, which was one of the reasons they'd broken up. However, Celia hadn't dated anyone since Liam. In my opinion, she was still pining for my brother.

"Your dad took the news of them using the pigs as a prank quite well," Trevor said.

Trevor had been in the house when Dustin, Noah, and Tessa apologized to Daddy. He hadn't yelled, nor had he gotten upset. Momma was the one who had been furious, especially with Tessa. I couldn't blame her either. Tessa had been a thorn in my side for most of my childhood and teenage years. She deserved the award for bully of the year, although Claire might not be far behind her.

I sipped my drink. "I'd rather not talk about pigs and Tessa. Where's Sloane these days?" I hadn't seen her that much in recent weeks, and when I had seen her at school, her head was buried in a book in the library. If we passed each other in the hall or cafeteria, she looked the other way.

"She's visiting Marcus this weekend."

I should've hitched a ride. I should be with Maiken. "I read your story that Celia published. I'm sorry about your mom."

His grin vanished in an instant. "Me too. Hey, I'll catch you later." Then he was gone.

I guess his mom hadn't been the right thing to bring up.

I was about to set my drink down when a hot breath breezed over my ear from behind. "Can I have this dance, babe?" His voice was raspy with the hint of a Southern drawl. I knew that voice well. It was a voice that made me swoon.

My stomach did a thousand somersaults. Maybe I was dreaming. Slowly, I turned, and tears shot out.

Maiken opened his arms. "Surprise." A slow, gorgeous grin emerged as his blue eyes glistened in the soft light.

I shook my head, blinking. Then I stepped up to him, and my hands slid up to touch his face. "Are you really here?"

His lips brushed over mine. "In the flesh."

"I thought—"

He took my drink from my hand and set it on the bar. Then his mouth crashed to mine, kissing me deeply.

I matched his kiss with so much emotion I couldn't breathe. I gave every ounce of love I had to Maiken in that moment. My night was complete.

He eased away slightly, sizing me up. "Wow! You look absolutely beautiful. I'm digging the short dress."

Fire pinched my cheeks. I was wearing a low-cut, above-the-knee gold flapper dress with spaghetti straps and gold heels to match. My hair was up and secured with a gold clip.

"You dressed for the occasion?" I asked, admiring how Maiken rocked his double-breasted suit and the way his sandy-blond hair was tucked behind his ears "I thought you didn't want to come."

He rolled his blue eyes. "Wherever you go, I go. Plus, I couldn't stand you up. Never, Quinn Thompson. You're my forever girl." He grabbed my hand. "Let's dance."

We skirted through the throng of kids until we found a spot on the dance floor. As soon as our bodies were molded together, I sagged in his arms. My night was complete. My heart was full, and I knew whatever the future held, Maiken would be there for me, and I for him.

He kissed me lightly on my ear. "Your mom looks as pretty as you."

I zeroed in on Momma, who was manning the food table across from the bar. She'd volunteered to chaperone after one of the parents had canceled at the last minute.

Maiken pressed his forehead to mine. "Not that much longer before we're out for the summer. I want to spend every minute I can with you."

I shuddered. Summers would never be the same for me, at least not the one coming up. I couldn't believe July was around the corner. I swore, every July, I would be reminded of my party and how everything around me had collapsed.

"We should go down the Cape for a couple of weeks," I said. "We can camp on the beach." Carter had done that last year with Brianna.

Celia and Noah bumped into us. "Maiken?" Celia's eyes widened. "You're here. Are you stealing my date?"

I giggled as Maiken tugged me closer.

The music stopped, and the head of the prom committee, Francine Dermott, tapped on the mike as her green gaze swept the room. "Hey, Kensington High, is everyone having a good time?"

The club erupted in shouts of "hell yeahs" and whistles.

"Let's give a big round of applause to everyone who had a hand in planning, setting up, and organizing this shindig."

More applause followed.

"Lastly, to the Smithtones." She waved a hand at the local band that played at several weddings and parties around the New England area.

Once the applause died down, Francine nodded at a dude on stage, wearing headphones. He pressed a couple of keys on his computer.

"Thanks to the media department, we've put together pictures and videos taken by the school's photographer and from those who sent in videos taken at venues like the science fair and other school events. Enjoy while the band takes a break. We'll be announcing king and queen later."

Sam Smith's voice crooned from the overhead speakers as the band headed off stage along with Francine.

Maiken wrapped an arm around my waist. "Let's go say hi to Kade."

I wanted to watch the slide show, not that I would be in any of the pictures. I'd hardly attended any school activities. But Celia had been one of the photographers, and I wanted to support my best friend. She'd worked hard all year, blogging, interviewing, and writing for the school's media and communications department.

"Just a second," I said to Maiken when the video began to play.

Celia sucked in a sharp breath, and Maiken went ramrod straight.

I blinked several times to make sure I wasn't seeing things.

My voice blared from the speakers, or more like my moans. "Let me."

A collective intake of breath zipped around the room as the video of Maiken and me played like a bad porno movie.

Oh my God!

Chapter 30

Quinn

I couldn't breathe. I couldn't get any air in my lungs. I dared not look at Momma. I could feel every pair of eyes glued to me as I watched the video play.

If Maiken was talking, I couldn't hear him.

Images of me strangling Trevor sprang to mind. But I'd deleted the video from his phone. I'd deleted it from the trash as well.

One muscle at a time, I swiveled my neck in search of Trevor Thames. Sloane had warned me. I was so stupid to believe he was a good guy.

I swallowed the dryness coating my throat. My limbs trembled as my breathing became labored.

"What is happening?" Maiken asked. "Who took this? I seriously will kill the fucker."

I'd never told Maiken about the video. I hadn't seen a reason to since I'd deleted it. I knew if I had, he would've done something stupid that would have gotten him kicked out of school and ruined his chances to play college basketball.

He let go of me and rushed up on stage. When he did, I swayed. Luckily, Celia was at my side to catch me. "Let's get out of here."

I couldn't get my tongue to work, let alone my legs. Why did I have bad luck at dances and large public gatherings?

Stupid me.

Whispers buzzed in the air. "That was kind of hot," someone nearby said.

"Who says Quinn is shy?" another said.

"Disgusting," one girl added.

A boy laughed. "Even good girls are bad. I love it."

"I wouldn't be able to show my face in school or ever if that were me," a mousy voice chimed in.

I swallowed a boulder as the room spun.

You only have a few weeks left. So no big deal. You'll walk away from high school and never look back.

The problem was I didn't want to be remembered as the hussy or whore. I didn't want to have the video be my defining moment. How could I get up on stage as valedictorian now? How could I stand before my senior class as the good girl, the perfect student with perfect grades and the perfect home?

I'd always been known as the shy one, the smart one, the one who wouldn't even think to yell or fight. I was the girl who'd always walked away or hidden in the shadows. But my senior year didn't scream any of those adjectives or acts. It screamed hussy, witch, fighter, and drunk. That was how kids would describe me when they looked back at their senior year.

Maiken tore something from the guy's computer, but the short, dark-haired boy who was in charge of the slideshow didn't protest. He lifted up his hands and said something to Maiken. My boyfriend stormed off stage, his features hard as he searched the room.

"Quinn." Celia's voice penetrated through the thick fog of hell in my head. "Let's leave."

I wasn't running. I wanted to give Trevor a piece of my mind. I couldn't let him do this to me and get away with it. For months, I'd been kind to him. I'd helped him with his studies. He'd been in my home and had dinner with my parents and me. He'd sat with Daddy and talked. They had watched basketball together. Daddy treated him like a son.

I clutched my chest, trying to get the stabbing pain to subside. His actions hurt more than the embarrassment gripping me. I'd thought we were friends. I dug deep for strength, set my jaw, and watched Maiken push through the crowd.

I tracked his movements as steam came out of his nose.

My gaze bounced off of him and onto Trevor, who stood ramrod straight. His skin was pale, and his eyes and mouth were wide open.

Voices hummed, and the word "fight" flew out of kids' mouths with eager anticipation as they watched the drama unfold.

I managed to get my legs to work. I couldn't let Maiken get into trouble.

The kids hovering around me gave me a wide berth as I marched up to Trevor and Maiken. But it wasn't the boys I was about to confront. The guilty party, who had a smug look painted on her not-so-pretty face, was Claire. She clung to Trevor, seemingly enjoying herself. In that moment, I wanted to tear into her like a lion who hadn't eaten in days.

Tessa popped out of the crowd, her shiny silver dress blinding me for a moment. "Quinn, don't do something you'll regret."

I laughed like a hysterical woman who had lost her mind. "Did you watch the same video I just did?" My voice was shockingly calm.

She gripped my shoulders. "It's grainy at best, and the only thing I saw was a girl who was making out with her boyfriend."

I snorted as I clenched my fists. "I was trying to tear off Maiken's clothes." I didn't even want to think about the moaning coming out of my mouth.

Someone in the crowd laughed. "You're hot, Quinn."

I growled. "Not helping."

Tessa shrugged. "Then go do something stupid." She opened her arm, waving me by. "You'll lose your valedictorian award."

I wanted to ask her why she cared. But I didn't have time to hash out why she was being nice to me. Maiken was glaring daggers at Claire, not Trevor.

I clenched my fists as I settled next to Maiken.

Claire puffed out her big chest. "Do you like your graduation gift?"

With every ounce of restraint I could muster, I said, "Thank you."

Claire inclined her head, pinching her eyebrows together. Apparently, that wasn't the reaction she was going for.

I had to be the bigger person. I would like to think I had matured, even though I was ready to tackle her to the floor. Tessa was right. I couldn't do something stupid. I'd worked too hard and been through hell to ensure I made valedictorian.

Trevor finally spoke. "You went into my computer? Unbelievable. We're through, Claire. I'm sick of your jealous rages."

Her brown eyes became basketballs, flickering with fire. "Why? Because you like her? You've been falling all over her feet since you met her. I don't get it." She gave me a disgusted sneer. "She's nothing. You'll regret this, Trev. Next year when it's just us in school, and Quinn isn't around, you'll be begging me to fuck you."

Maiken reared back. "Wait. This is your doing?" he asked Trevor. "You filmed Quinn and me?"

The club was completely silent as kids watched intently.

Trevor blew out a breath. "I didn't do it for malicious intent. It was a stupid thing to do."

"I erased it from his phone," I mumbled.

Maiken gaped. "You knew about this?" Disappointment and hurt swam in his blue eyes.

My heart plummeted. "He showed me, and then he let me delete it from his phone. I didn't tell you because it was a nonissue."

He opened his hand. "Um… This thumb drive says otherwise."

Kade's deep voice resonated. "Okay, let's break this up. Back to having a good time, or else I'll be forced to shut the party down."

Momma rushed up. "What's going on?"

I expelled every ounce of air I had in my lungs. The food table was tucked on the other side of the bar and not in Momma's line of sight. So I was thankful she hadn't seen me up on the big screen, although she had to have heard my voice.

"Your daughter is a whore," Claire said.

Momma raised her hand, but I caught it before she did something stupid. "Mom, I can handle this."

My body warmed at how Momma was ready to defend me.

"Young lady," Momma said to Claire. "I suggest you leave my presence before I do something you won't like."

Trevor grabbed Claire's arm. "Let's go. Mrs. Thompson, I apologize." Trevor practically dragged Claire out of Momma's view.

"Now tell me what happened," Momma said to me in her motherly tone that was equal parts scary and concerning.

I wasn't about to tell her anything in front of a crowd full of kids. Thankfully, the band returned to the stage and launched into an upbeat song. Kids dispersed, and some started dancing since a fight wasn't imminent.

Maiken entwined his fingers with mine and pulled me through the club as we followed Momma. Kade stood at the door of the storeroom, holding it open for us. He had a knowing look in his copper eyes as though he'd been in my shoes.

Once we were behind closed doors with the music muted, Momma stuck her hands on her hips. "What happened out there?"

Maiken let go of my hand, watching me with as much concern as Momma had.

There was no sense in lying to Momma. She would find out anyway.

"Claire, the girl you told to leave, leaked a video of Maiken and me in a compromising position." My gaze was glued to my strappy gold heels, because I was afraid to see the disappointment in Momma's eyes.

"As in a sex video?" Momma was on the verge of screaming at the top of her lungs.

I shook my head, still not meeting her eyes. "Not really. I was unbuckling Maiken's jeans, and—"

"Don't finish that sentence. I don't want to know." Fury threaded through her words. "Do you know what that could do to your college and future employment if that got out on the web, Quinn? And you, Maiken. How could you let this happen? Your basketball career could go up in smoke."

Maiken cleared his throat. "Ma'am, the video was dark and grainy, and we weren't naked. I also have the evidence." He held up the thumb drive.

I cringed at the word "naked." What if we had been? I'd been so flipping stupid to drink.

"It's my fault, Momma. That was the night of my party, and well, I wasn't thinking straight."

Someone knocked on the door, and then Trevor came in. "Can we talk?" He addressed all of us, holding his head high. "I know 'sorry' doesn't cut the mustard." He cupped his hands in front of him, his expression dour. "When I first arrived in Ashford, my world had been turned upside down. A new town. A strange home. A new school. My dad thought a fresh start would temper the memories of my mom's death. He got on with his life like she didn't even exist." He took a breath as he kept his focus on Momma.

I found a crate to sit on. Maiken didn't move from his spot near a shelf of toilet paper.

"I was furious with him," Trevor continued. "I lashed out any chance I had. That night when Sloane said she was going to a party, I followed her to the farm. I was walking around the property when I spotted you two." He looked at Maiken and me. "I had no intentions of malice. I film a lot of things."

"You saved it on your computer, though," I said. "And you failed to tell me that part."

"When I hooked my phone to my computer that night to charge it —like I do on most nights—my photos and videos download automatically. Honestly, I didn't even think about that when you deleted the video from my phone."

Maybe I was crazy, but I believed him.

"And Claire?" Maiken asked. "Does she normally go snooping into your things?"

"She hates Quinn, man. I'm sorry about what Claire did. I will wipe the video off my computer. If you want to watch me, I'm cool with that." He addressed Momma. "Ma'am, please forgive me. You and your husband have been kind and like a second family to me."

Momma grasped his arms. "Son, I appreciate your honesty. You're a good boy. And I'm so very sorry about your mom. You have a home with us at any time."

"You're not going to fire me?" he asked, seemingly holding his breath, looking like he was about to lose it.

"Everyone deserves a second chance," Momma said. "But I want you to learn from this." She wagged her finger at each of us. "All of you. Intimacy between two people belongs behind closed doors." She gave me a pointed look. "I also hope, young lady, you've learned some valuable lessons this year."

My heart was beating out of my chest as I waited for the bomb to drop. I just knew she was about to ground me or tell Daddy what I'd done.

As if she was in my head, she said, "We will not speak of this to your father. However, the three of you will make sure there is not another piece of evidence of the video. I would hate to see it surface years down the line when you're trying to get a job."

"I promise, Mrs. Thompson," Trevor said. "I will erase it."

"You will," Maiken finally piped in. A smidge of fear washed over him. "If not, I will do whatever it takes to make sure you don't get into a college basketball program."

Trevor's Adam's apple bobbed. "We'll do it together, man."

"Good," Momma said. "Now, I'm going to return to my post. I'll see you at home, Quinn." Then she walked out.

Trevor apologized once more then walked out, hanging his head.

Once Maiken and I were alone, I bent over and held my knees, blowing out a ton of air. "I hate high school."

Maiken glared at me. "How come you didn't tell me?"

I straightened. "I didn't tell anyone because I was embarrassed and mortified."

"With me?"

"No, of course not. With myself." I grabbed his hands. "I did something under the influence. You told me to stop. You even thought someone was watching us, and I didn't listen. I was mad at myself. When Trevor let me delete the video from his phone, I thought that was the end of it. I wasn't thinking about where else he could've stored it. I was only thinking about how I dodged a bullet. Because if Trevor had turned out to be the creep I thought he was and the video went viral, then you might not have gotten the offer letter from BC." I might've been reaching on that one.

"Maybe," Maiken said. "But it hurts to know you didn't tell me."

A pang of anguish clutched my chest. "I love you, Maiken Maxwell, to the stars and back. I promise I will never keep anything from you again. Ever. I swear on Daddy's heart."

He cupped my face with one hand, and I leaned into his touch. The warm, gentle, soothing, and loving gesture sewed my emotions back together.

"From this day forward," he said, "we are partners through thick, thin, highs, lows, and everything in between. No secrets. No lies. We support each other. We tell each other everything. Because someday, Quinn Thompson, you'll be my wife. I will marry you."

A swarm of butterflies went wild inside me. "My heart is yours, Maiken Maxwell. It's yours to keep forever."

He brushed his lips over mine before he kissed me, slow, wet, and sensual.

He was the love of my life, and he was spot-on. I would marry him someday.

Chapter 31

Quinn

The energy in the air was electric. The senior class occupied the front half of the gymnasium while I sat on stage, looking out at a sea of blue and gold caps and gowns. Two hundred seniors would walk across the stage in about thirty minutes, their pulses beating hard as they stood tall and smiled broadly.

Our teenage years were coming to a close—the fun times, the bad times, the drama, sporting events, tests, and everything else that came with being a teenager. But like my peers, I was proud of myself. I was proud that I'd made it through the awkward stages, the bullies, the long nights before exams, the parties I seriously wanted to erase from my memory, and most of all for turning into a strong individual.

As I half listened to Principal Sanders address our graduating class, I thought back to the first day I walked into Kensington during my freshman year. I'd been scared, timid, and excited. The last four years had been a series of firsts. My first crush. My first boyfriend. My first kiss. My first argument with Maiken. And my first time with a boy I loved.

Nerves churned in my stomach. I was about to make my first public speech in front of an audience with my parents, my brothers, my boyfriend, my close friends, and peers. I'd never addressed an audience that big. I wasn't even sure if words would come out of my mouth.

As the principal droned on, I recited my speech in my head. I'd been practicing it for the last two weeks in front of a mirror, to Maiken, to Celia, and to Momma. When I'd first started writing my speech, I had one message in mind: work hard and prosper. But I had changed my tune after the prom. Now I had a different theme in mind.

Speaking of the prom, the backlash hadn't been as severe as I'd thought it would be. Claire had been nonexistent. Celia had learned that Claire had gotten a one-day suspension. Francine, the head of the prom committee, had made sure Claire paid. I couldn't exactly encourage Principal Sanders to punish Claire given my actions in the video.

I felt that I was as much at fault as Claire had been. If I hadn't gotten drunk, then the video would've never happened. Luckily for me, the principal hadn't mentioned a word about the prom incident to me. I'd been quite nervous she would, but my actions hadn't hurt anyone or broken any rules on school property. The only thing that had been broken was my pride. In addition, Maiken and I had made darn sure Trevor erased all digital copies of the video from his computer, and he'd been very accommodating and apologetic.

"Now I would like to give the podium over to our valedictorian, Quinn Thompson." Principal Sanders turned and nodded to me as she clapped along with the entire audience.

I took in a quick breath, hoping to calm my nerves, and rose, smiling at her as I walked up to the podium. My pulse beat a staccato rhythm as I placed my note cards on the podium and looked out at the students.

"Focus on one person," Mrs. Flowers had said. "Give your speech like you're having a casual conversation with that person."

I swallowed, lifted my chin, and cleared my throat as I adjusted the mike. My hands were trembling as I searched for someone to latch onto. I wanted Maiken to be sitting in the front row, but he was somewhere in the back. But when I swept my gaze to my right, Maiken was standing in the aisle along the wall, smiling warmly and proudly.

I briefly closed my eyes, feeling a sense of relief that I had him to support me.

"Fellow graduates, it's been four years of firsts and lasts." *Definitely firsts with Maiken, but never lasts.* "Four years of learning and growing. And as our high school days come to an end, we should be proud of what we've accomplished." I scanned my peers before continuing. "We owe a debt of gratitude to those who have helped us get here today. The teachers who have worked tirelessly, giving their free time to support extracurricular activities, clubs, sports, and the list goes on. Our illustrious guidance counselor, Mrs. Flowers, who has gone out of her way to help us as we prepare for college. To Principal Sanders, who has always made sure we have the best state-of-the-art tools to help us learn and to keep us on the straight and narrow." I took a breath and swallowed. "Let's give them a round of applause."

Once the audience was done clapping, I soldiered on. "I stand before you today not only as your valedictorian but also as your peer and friend." I held my head high. "What I tell you now isn't from these note cards." I tapped my heart. "My message to you comes right from here. Don't be afraid to take a chance. Don't be afraid to do something you think you can't do. We are strong. We are powerful. We are ready to take on new challenges."

Most of the heads in the audience nodded and bobbed.

"Since I was a little girl, my dad"—I glanced to my left and homed in on my dad, who was sitting two rows up next to my mom—"my dad always told me, 'You will do great things one day, Quinn.'" Tears threatened as my dad beamed at me. "I believe each and every one of you will do great things. We are now armed with the tools we need to grab our dreams by the horns. We are ready to adapt, grow even more, learn, love, and build a world where one day our kids will be as proud as my parents are of me right this minute." Tears flowed down my cheeks. "So with that, I would like to leave you with one last thing." I puffed out my chest and opened my arms. "The future is your playground. Use it to have the best darn time of your life."

The senior class of Kensington High, along with parents and loved ones, gave me a standing ovation.

I smiled through a cloud of tears, and for the first time in all my years, I wasn't afraid of life after high school. I was ready to take on

whatever was thrown my way, and I knew without a doubt that I would
do great things.

Epilogue

Maiken

In one week, Quinn and I were off to Boston College. In one week, we would begin our new life as college students. If anyone asked me a year ago where I thought I would be, my answer would've been, "I'm not sure."

My senior year of high school wasn't what I'd imagined. I'd never expected to be at a new school, away from Mom, away from Quinn. But I wouldn't have changed a thing. I believed that year had given me a chance to grow up, to see the world in a different light, to focus on my dreams, and above all else, to deepen my love for Quinn. Not seeing her every day hadn't been easy. But I believed we were stronger because of the separation. I believed that she and I could do anything now. Our relationship was impenetrable. We had each other through thick and thin.

"Maiken!" Quinn shouted. "Pay attention."

I chuckled as I focused on my beautiful goddess. She was trying to get me on a horse, and after almost three years of telling her no, I'd decided to slay one of my demons. I'd been around horses since I met Quinn, and they weren't as scary anymore.

She held out the reins. "It's simple. Apple is kind and gentle. Don't be afraid."

"I'll be fine," I said as Apple wagged her tail.

I slipped my foot into a stirrup as I took hold of the reins and lifted myself up onto the saddle.

Quinn clapped, and she lit up like a Christmas tree. "See, you're a natural."

If I got to see her smiling and happy, I would climb up and onto a hundred horses for her.

I inhaled the afternoon summer air. A light breeze ruffled my hair. It was the perfect day for a trot through the woods. Our plan was to explore, but I had other things in mind once Quinn and I were deep in the woods.

Like the horse expert she was, she mounted Lightning effortlessly. The black horse inched forward as though he weren't used to someone riding him.

Quinn petted his neck. "It's okay, boy. We'll run soon."

I wasn't about to full-out gallop. But it would be fun to see Quinn fly with her horse.

"Okay," Quinn said. "You ready. You remember what I taught you?"

"Hold on to the reins for dear life," I teased.

She rolled her amber eyes. "Silly. Apple will follow me. But if you want her to move faster, just dig your heels into her."

I gave her the thumbs-up. "Lead the way, Goddess."

She giggled as she took off on a trail along the perimeter of the farm.

Before long, we were in the thick of the woods, and I was surprisingly fine with how Apple trotted as though she were smelling every branch and leaf along the way.

That sense of fear I'd had for horses diminished greatly. I was actually digging how freeing riding a horse was making me feel.

Quinn led the way for about twenty minutes until we came out of the dense thicket. The Maxwell Lake lay before us.

She beamed at me as she climbed off Lightning. "Are you good?"

"Never better," I said as I tried to get off Apple like an expert rider. But my foot got caught in the stirrup, and I faltered.

Quinn gasped, rushing to catch up.

I laughed as I managed to get two feet on the ground. "I'm cool."

She giggled. "You still don't like horses. Do you?"

I clutched her waist. "What I do like is you and me and..."

She squealed. "Let's jump in." She removed her tank top, revealing a yellow bikini top. "We have the lake all to ourselves."

That we did. My cousin Kade's house was across the lake, but I doubted he would be watching us.

We secured the horses to a tree before Quinn took off, diving into the water.

I tore off my shirt and chased after her.

Once we were both in the cool lake water, she locked her hands around my neck and her legs around my waist.

"Are you ready for college?" she asked as I twirled us around.

I was more than ready. I couldn't wait to play college ball. I couldn't wait to begin my new life with her at my side.

I pecked her on the lips. "I am, but right now, I want you."

She slid off me. "Then you'll have to catch me." She started swimming, but not that fast.

"I will always catch you, Quinn Thompson. Forever and ever." As I swam up to her, I was on top of the world. I had the most beautiful, confident, intelligent, and amazing girl a boy could ever have.

We were both ready to begin anew, and as she'd said in her valedictorian speech, "The future is your playground. Use it to have the best darn time of your life."

I planned on doing just that with her.

DON'T MISS OUT

Bestselling author **S.B. Alexander** writes young adult and new adult romances that span the sub-categories of coming of age, sports, paranormal, suspense, and military fiction. Her writing is emotional, angsty, and character driven. She's best known for The Maxwell and The Maxwell Family Saga series.

S.B. or Susan as she likes to be called is a navy veteran, former high school teacher, and former corporate sales executive. She's a lover of sports, especially baseball, although nowadays you can find her glued to the TV during football season.

When she's not writing, she's a full-time caregiver to her soul mate of twenty-one years who got a bad deal in life when he was diagnosed with ALS. Her motto: "Life is too short to waste. So live every moment like it's your last."

You can connect with S.B. Alexander in the following ways:
Reader Group: http://sbalexander.com/sbareaderroom
Author Website: http://sbalexander.com
Newsletter: http://sbalexander.com/newsletter
Email: susan@sbalexander.com

<u>NEVER MISS A NEW RELEASE:</u>
Follow S.B. Alexander on Amazon
Follow S.B. Alexander on BookBub

facebook.com/sbalexander.authorpage
twitter.com/sbalex_author
instagram.com/sbalexanderauthor
amazon.com/author/sbalexander
bookbub.com/authors/s-b-alexander
goodreads.com/sbalexander

ALSO BY S.B. ALEXANDER

THE MAXWELL SERIES

Upper Young Adult/New Adult Contemporary Romance

Dare to Kiss

Dare to Dream

Dare to Love

Dare to Dance

Dare to Live

Dare to Breathe

Dare to Embrace

The Kade & Lacey Collection Box Set

Dare to Kiss Coloring Book Companion

THE MAXWELL FAMILY SAGA SERIES

Young Adult Contemporary Romance

My Heart to Touch

My Heart to Hold

My Heart to Give

My Heart to Keep*

STANDALONES

New Adult Contemporary Romance

Unforgettable

Breaking Rules

Rescuing Riley

Holding On To Forever

THE HART SERIES

New Adult Romantic Suspense

Hart of Darkness

Hart of Vengeance

Hart of Redemption*

THE VAMPIRE SEAL SERIES

Young Adult Paranormal Romance

On the Edge of Humanity

On the Edge of Eternity

On the Edge of Destiny

On the Edge of Misery

On the Edge of Infinity

The Vampire SEAL Collection

*Coming Soon.

Visit http://sbalexander.com for all future release dates. Please note release dates are subject to change based on reader demand and the author's schedule. Subscribing to the author's newsletter or following her on Facebook is the best way to stay updated with planned new releases.